STORMY ENCOUNTERS

Short Stories

TWISTED
Capella Family (Book 1)

REIGN
Capella Family (Book 2)

LOST SOUL
Warriors MC (Book 1)

A MIDNIGHT REVELATION
Warriors MC (Book 2)

LOVE UNLEASHED
Elemental's MC

ONE SMALL SPANISH WISH

https://alexiferreirawrite.wixsite.com/mysite

Amazon.com/author/alexiferreira

Facebook.com/alexiferreira.writer

Readers Group -
https://www.facebook.com/groups/3099856723403202

Contents

DOM 1 4

LOLA 2...13

DOM 3 21

LOLA 4...29

DOM 5 39

LOLA 6...48

DOM 7 57

LOLA 8...67

DOM 9 76

Reign 85

AMORE 1...86

GINO 2 90

AMORE 3...96

GINO 4 104

AMORE 5...111

GINO 6 124

RAINE 1 128

DAMIEN 2 134

RAINE 3 139

DAMIEN 4 145

RAINE 5 152

DAMIEN 6 157

ELLA 1 166

ZEN 02...177

ELLE 3...187

ZEN 4..199

DRACO 1 206

KATRINA 2 215

DRACO 3 224

KATRINA 4 237

DRACO 5 248

KATRINA 6 259

One Small Spanish Wish.......................................273

ALORA 1 274

JASON 2..280

ALORA 3 287

JASON 4..298

A MESSAGE FROM ALEXI FERREIRA 310

TWISTED

Capella Family (Book 1)

DOM 1

"Dom, Alfredo is here."

Shit, he better have my money if he's interrupting me now. I look at Tina on her knees before me, her dyed blonde hair dishevelled from my fingers, her hands on my waistband, unbuttoning them. I look over my shoulder at Blade as he stands leaning against the door, waiting for my reply.

"Does he have my money?" I pull my hands away from Tina's hair to take hold of her wrists, stopping her from rubbing her hands over my crotch.

"No."

"What the fuck? So why are you bothering me?" I see Blade's smirk as he inclines his head towards the front of the restaurant.

"You are going to want to talk to him. He has a deal I think you are going to find interesting."

Alfredo is deep in debt. I have been giving him chance after chance to pay me back, but he has failed to meet the deadline every time. Now he has a deal. It better be a fucking good deal for the amount he owes.

"Stop," I mutter as Tina lowers her head, trying to move her mouth over my zipped-up slacks. "Get up. Leave."

"Aww, Dom, come on, let them wait," she says in her irritating voice as she pouts her smudged red-painted lips at me.

"Move. I don't feel like it anymore," I mutter as I let go of her wrists and take hold of her upper arms, helping her up so that I can get up from my dark-brown leather chair. I hear her mutter but pay her no attention as I tuck in my shirt and look at Blade. He is my right-hand man and one person I trust with my life. We grew up together, into this life of crime. Blade could have left when my father died, but he decided to stay and become my right-hand man.

Becoming the boss of the Capella family at the age of twenty-seven was my first challenge, as most of the men thought me too young to carry this responsibility, but I soon won their trust by tripling our income. Some have challenged me, but they don't live long to make the same mistake again. I learned at an early age that being in the mafia is a game of either kill or be killed.

Familia is everything to me. We fight, we make up, but we always stay truthful with each other.

Tina walks past me in her tiny dress and spiky heels, glaring at Blade as she exits. "What do you see in her?" Blade asks as he saunters in.

"Did you come here to speak about my sex life, or why you interrupted me?" I place my hand at my waist, waiting for an update.

"As I said, Alfredo is outside, and he has the deal of the century for you." I can see by his grin that he's not going to elaborate.

"You're not going to tell me what it is, are you?" I shake my head in annoyance. Sometimes it's not good being friends with your right-hand man. "One of these days, I'm going to shoot you," I threaten as I make my way out of my office, only to hear him chuckling behind me.

I walk down the corridor, past the kitchen that is still closed at this time, as it's only ten in the morning, and into the dining area. I stop as I see Alfredo standing near the door. It is clear that he is nervous. Whatever this deal is, he isn't sure I will accept it.

"Alfredo." He jumps in fright when he hears my voice, snapping around to face me. "I hear you have a business proposition for me."

"Dom, yes, yes, I do." I know Big Mac would have frisked him when he walked in, so this nervousness can only be that he's not sure about what he's offering.

"Come sit with me, Alfredo." I incline my head towards my table set in the corner with a view of the entire restaurant. Sliding into my chair, I wait for Alfredo to take the seat before me. He must be in his late forties, early fifties, and ever since I can remember, Alfredo has borrowed money from us. He usually pays it back, but this time, he seems to be having problems.

"Talk to me, Alfredo. Why are you having such difficulty in paying back the money this time?" I know he has a gambling problem. That is why when it gets to a certain amount, his tab is frozen and he has to pay back what he owes, but this time, we had to help him with an extra ten thousand because he went to ask for money somewhere else and they were threatening to kill him.

"I just can't seem to get on top of things."

"Did you go get help like I told you to last time?" When he came to ask for more money, I told him that I would only help him if he got help with his addiction. I know that sometimes I'm too lenient with some of them, but a dead man doesn't pay his bills.

"I did, I swear," he says. Placing his hand in his pocket, he takes out a piece of paper for me to see. I nod, seeing the confirmation that he has been seeing someone.

"Fine, then what is this deal you want to propose to me?" I lean back, crossing my arms, waiting for his reply.

"I don't think I will ever be able to get enough money to pay you back, Dom." I frown at his statement. The only thing that interests me is money. Whatever this deal is, it better be a way of paying back all the money he owes. "That is why I thought of this way to pay you back. It is the most precious thing to me." If he gives me a watch or jewellery, I swear I will shoot him myself for wasting my time.

"Get to it, Alfredo. Time is money." I'm not a very patient man, and his dawdling is starting to irritate me.

"I want you to have Lola to pay for my debt." I tense. Isn't Lola his wife? I glance over at Blade to see him grinning.

"What am I supposed to do with your wife?" I see Alfredo's shocked expression at my outburst. He might think his wife is the best thing since pastrami, but I doubt anyone else will, as I'm sure she isn't a spring chicken any longer.

"Wife? No, no, Lola is not my wife," Alfredo says. "Lola is my daughter." I glare over at Blade as his shoulders shake with laughter.

"Alfredo, what am I supposed to do with your daughter. I'm not into prostitution." I shake my head in frustration. I hate it when people reach a point where they will go to any lengths to save their skin. This Lola doesn't deserve being sold like this by her father.

"No, not prostitution, but she is beautiful. She can work here in the restaurant or at one of your clubs serving. She is a hard worker. She will pay off my debt."

Sure. At the salary the waitresses earn, the debt will be paid in ten years.

"Does your daughter even know that you are trying to sell her to me?" I can't mask the disgust I feel for him. A man who will sell his own daughter is very low in my books. The Capella family is all about *familia*. To come to me to try to sell his daughter is asking to be dead.

"No, but I promise you she will do as I say."

I shake my head in disbelief. I would never have thought this of him.

"How old is Lola?" I shouldn't care, but I do. If I say no, he might go make this offer to someone else to try to get the money he needs.

Alfredo leans forward as he pulls his wallet out of his back pocket. Opening the wallet, he pulls out what looks like a photo and hands it to me. I look down at the photo and frown. This is his daughter? He wasn't joking when he said she is beautiful.

"She is now twenty-three." She has stunning dark-brown hair that flows down past her shoulders. Her smiling eyes are looking straight at whoever is taking the photo, and at first, I thought she had brown eyes, but they are actually a dark blue that look dark because of the lighting. Her skin looks to be an olive tone, enhancing her Latin descendance.

I look up at Alfredo and see him looking at the photo lovingly. Why would a man who seems to love his daughter submit himself to doing this? "If Lola agrees to this idea of yours, I want you to bring her here and I will talk to her. Only after my discussion with her will I decide."

"No prostitution," he says.

"You are starting to work on my very last nerve," I grunt, irritated that he still has the audacity to try to set rules. "You can leave." He hesitates before he sees my angry expression. He quickly rises from his chair, jumping in surprise when he finds Blade standing right behind him.

"Oh, I didn't see you."

Blade inclines his head towards the exit, which quickly has Alfredo making his way there. Blade slides into Alfredo's empty seat and just sits there, looking at me.

"What?" I ask, irritated.

"Are you really considering it?"

"If we don't take her, he will go sell her to the next highest bidder."

Blade raises a brow. "So?"

"It's not her fault that her father has gambled her life away," I mutter. Raising my hand, I rub at my tense jaw.

"Where are you going to put her?" I hadn't thought about that yet, but we have businesses all over the city. I am sure we can slot her in somewhere.

"Well, seeing as you are so amused with the situation, I will leave it up to you to find her a place."

Blade grins as he shakes his head in amusement. "It helps that she's pretty, doesn't it?"

"Have you seen her?" I'm sure I would have remembered if I had ever seen Lola somewhere. This is the first time I've seen her.

Blade shakes his head, his grin widening. "No, but I saw your face when you looked at her photo. I knew then that you would be suckered into taking her." Blade shakes his head exaggeratedly. "A pretty woman is going to be your downfall."

"All women are pretty in their own way," I mutter, shrugging as I stand.

"You just have way too many of them for your own good," Blade teases.

"Look who's talking. I don't see you going to bed alone every night." Blade and I are similar in height, and we both have dark-brown hair and brown eyes, but that is where the resemblance ends. I have a scar across my eyebrow and up over my forehead that I acquired when still a teenager when I thought I was all powerful. This scar helps me remember that no matter who you are, there is always someone better than you out there. You mustn't assume, and always be sure before going into a situation.

"Enough of this. Have you heard from Joey yet?" We heard that the Ukrainians were dealing on our turf. I keep my streets clean; I don't want any drugs where we live. If they start dealing here, then we start having problems, and I don't want problems.

Joey went to speak to his contacts to find out if what we heard is true. If it is, then we have a problem, because I won't let anyone deal here. Joey grew up with us, but he is two years younger and, as such, has always worked to try to fit in with the two of us. While Blade and I have already turned thirty, Joey is still twenty-eight.

"The last I heard was last night when he texted me saying that he was meeting his contact this morning." I lift my arm to look at my wristwatch—nearly midday.

"Phone h—" I'm interrupted from telling Blade to phone Joey when I see Vito running inside.

"He's been shot," he yells from the entrance, pointing behind him. "Joey is taking him to the ER."

"Who?" I ask when I reach him. Vito is the youngest out of all of us and a hot head, but his heart is in the right place. He and Joey are brothers; you don't usually see one without the other.

"It's Gino. They fucking shot Gino." Gino started to hang around with us when he was a teenager. His parents and sister were gunned down before his eyes. He was the only one to survive. His aunt took him in, and when he started to get into trouble with the wrong crowd, she asked my father if he would keep an eye on him.

"How is he?"

"Don't know. There was so much blood," Vito says as he pulls his fingers through his hair.

"Who shot him, Vito?" Blade asks as he stands next to me.

"The fucking Ukrainian shot him; we were driving back when Gino saw one of them dealing. We stopped, and Gino got out to talk to him. Before Gino could even reach him, he pulled out his weapon and fired at him." This problem has just become real. They threatened my people, hurt them. They will now deal with the Capella family.

LOLA 2

My feet are killing me. All I want to do is get home and fall into bed. I look around to find a seat on the bus. At this time, it's not too full, but sometimes you still find weirdos, so I always try to sit next to another woman or a respectable-looking man. Tonight, I'm in luck, as I see Dolores siting in her usual seat.

I have been taking this same bus for the last year and a half, and most times, I see the same people on it. Dolores is one of them. She must be in her early fifties, and from previous conversations, she works in a shoe factory. I enjoy our chats even when she tries to set me up with her son.

"Hi, Dolores. How are you tonight?" I say as I take the seat next to her.

"Good. No use complaining, is there?" she says with a smile as she pats my leg. "How was college tonight?"

"It's okay. I'm nearly finished, which is good. Maybe I can find a proper job." I have been working at a diner, opening in the mornings, and then just after lunchtime, I go to college, where I'm studying accounting. Today, the diner was extra busy, and then college just dragged, which is why I'm so tired tonight, but first, I need to shower, as I won't have time in the morning, and then if Papa hasn't eaten, I will have to make him something quick.

"You're a good girl. I always tell my boy he must get a girl like you, not those skanky girls he gets." She pulls a face, which has me smiling. She has told me that her son works in one of the clubs in town as a bouncer. A Capella-family club. Just the name has my anger rising. They own most of the businesses and most probably have their fingers in the others. If it weren't for them, everything would have been different, but instead, my mama died before her time because of working herself to the bone, and my papa is a broken shell of a man who gambles his life away.

If they didn't keep feeding his addiction by lending him money all the time, money that we struggle to pay back, then my mother might still be alive and I wouldn't have to work and go to college and then go home to a dismal house that just brings me bad memories.

"Well, here's my stop. Take care, sweetheart." Dolores's words bring me back to the present. I smile as she leaves. The next stop will be mine, and then another five minutes and I'll be home. Stepping out of the bus, I make my way up the street where I used to play as a kid. A time when I was still carefree, not realizing what was going on.

I know something is wrong the minute I open the door and see Papa standing at the entrance to the sitting room, waiting for me. By his red-rimmed eyes, I can tell he's been weeping. "Papa, what's wrong?" I drop my haversack on the floor. Closing the door behind me, I rush towards him.

"Lola, I'm so sorry," he says as he places his arms around me to pull me closer to him. His familiar smell engulfs me. No matter all the heartache he has brought me, he is still my father. What he has is an illness, and family doesn't leave family when they are ill.

"You are worrying me, Papa. What's wrong? Tell me." I lean back to look at his face, seeing the tears coursing down his cheeks. He has never been strong; my mother was the one who kept him on the right path, but since her death, he has been lost.

"There was no other way. I had to do it." His ramblings are worrying. Knowing my father, he could have done anything.

"Come, Papa, let's go sit down, and then you can tell me everything. It will be okay, you will see." I take his hand, pulling him behind me. I sit on the couch, pulling gently at his arm until he sits down next to me. "Now, tell me what you did."

He places his elbows on his knees, his head in his hands. He is the picture of a defeated man, a man who has given up on life. He works in a factory that produces car parts, and has been with them ever since he was a teenager, growing into a foreman position. He is a good man. He is just lost.

"I owe the Capella family money."

I close my eyes, wondering how much he has gotten himself into this time. "How much, Papa? We will find a way to pay them." I don't know what else I can sell. Looking around, I see the empty walls, the threadbare couches. The box TV because we haven't had money to buy a flat screen. The rest of the house is pretty much the same.

"We can't. It's a lot. That's why I had to do it."

"Okay, Papa, let's start there. Do what? What did you do to pay off your debt?"

"I told Dom you would work for him to pay off the debt."

I tense. "What? Work for the Capella family? No way. You know how I feel about them. I will not work for that man." I snap up off the couch; how can he tell that man that I will work for him? "And what exactly is he expecting me to do?" There is no way I will sell my body for money; how can my father even do this?

"Just what you are doing at the diner, nothing more, and that diner is a dump. You know the Capella family takes care of their employees. It's a good deal, Lola, for everyone."

Of course he would say that. It's not him working for them.

"They are criminals, Papa. I will not be working for criminals." I start to pace. There must be another way to pay this money he owes. "How much this time, Papa?" He finally lifts his head to look at me. I can see by his expression that I'm not going to like the answer.

"Fifty thousand," he murmurs. The figure has me stopping in shock. He has never owed so much. What am I going to do? Where can I go and get that much money?

"But I thought they had a cut-off? How did you get to fifty?" I ask, still in shock; I can't believe the amount.

"They do, but I asked from someone else, and they threatened to kill me when I couldn't pay, so Dom paid them off, but now I have to pay Dom." Shit, I don't want to know that the bloodsucker actually had a heart and tried to save my papa's life. "I'm seeing someone. Dom only gave me the money if I found help. I won't do it again, Lola."

How many times have I heard this before? My mother got him to seek help before, and it didn't help. Nothing helps.

Why would the Capella boss want him to seek help? I mean, it's good for him when people like my father exist. That doesn't make sense. There must be some obscure reason he made that a condition to giving my dad the money.

"Maybe I can find a second job." I don't know when I would be able to fit it in. If I could just have another two months to finish my studies, then I could work two jobs. I really don't want to drop out now when I am so close to finishing.

"You don't need a second job, Lola. You can even study while you work for Dom. It is a good thing, *figlia*." He stands and places his hands on my shoulders. "I know you don't like the Capella family, but they take care of their own. If you start working for them, you can grow in one of their businesses, maybe do the accounts for the one you work for." I'm sure the Capella family has a team of accountants who sort out all their businesses. They are not going to need someone who just came out of college to do their books, but I won't tell him that, as he seems to think he's doing me a favour.

"Let me think about it, but if I think of a way to pay them, you will agree with me." He doesn't say anything for a minute, but then he nods and hugs me close.

"I'm sorry I'm such a disappointment." I can hear the pain in his tone, and I want to deny it, but I can't. He does disappoint me, but I have faith that one day, he will stop and become the man he can be. I just wish my mom could be here to see it.

"Have you eaten?" I ask as I step back.

"I'm not hungry, but thank you. Why don't you go take a nice shower and then sleep? You look tired." He gently strokes a finger over my cheek like he used to when I was a little girl and I was upset. "I love you, Lola," he says, a tear running down his cheek.

"I know, Papa. I love you too." I stand on my tiptoes and kiss his cheek tenderly before stepping back and making my way to my room. Well, I never expected this today, but one thing I have learned in my young age is to roll with the punches. Now I just need to try to find a way to pay all that money back. How can I possibly come up with fifty thousand? How can he even spend that much money without having anything to show for it?

Looking around my room, I sigh. There is nothing here worth anything. I don't have any jewellery, as everything my mother had at one time or another she sold to pay for my father's debts. I close the door behind me. Walking towards my bed, I sit.

I promised my mother before she died that I would look after my papa, but as time goes by, it is becoming more and more difficult to help him. This time, he has offered my services to pay his debts. What will be next? He says he is seeing someone to try to get help; how long will this time last? How long can I carry on doing this, paying for his mistakes without it killing me like it killed my mother?

I hear my phone beep. Pulling it out of my jacket pocket, I groan when I see a message from Dina. Dina is my cousin, and we have been the best of friends since we were born. She sent me a message this morning, and with one thing and another, I forgot to message her back. Pressing the call button, I bring the phone to my ear and wait.

"I thought you didn't want to talk to me," she teases. Dina is the type of person who is always trying to make those around her happy, lots of times forgetting about herself in the process. She will go out of her way to help those close to her.

"Sorry, I got your message just as I started work. Then I completely forgot until now when you sent me your text."

"It's okay, I know you don't love me as much as I love you," she teases. "Anyway, how about it? Are you going to come out with me tomorrow night?" I completely forgot that tomorrow is Saturday. No college, but I have an assignment due next week.

"I have work in the morning, and then I have an assignment I need to start."

"Oh, come on, how long has it been since you've been out? You can't work all the time, Lola. Besides, you can start the assignment on Sunday."

"I will let you know tomorrow after work, okay? But now I need to shower and then sleep, because otherwise, you're going to be talking and I'm going to be snoring in your ear."

She laughs. "You work too much, Lola; you need to rest more. I'm going to let you escape and have your shower and beauty sleep, but think about tomorrow, okay?"

"Okay, night," I murmur as I stand. I have been so tired lately that I haven't even gone out in such a long time, and now with this debt pending over my head, I have a feeling I'm going to be more tired than before, but family is family, and there is nothing more important than family.

DOM 3

"They need to pay, Dom. We can't let them get away with this," Vito says as he stops the car in front of the restaurant. We have been to the hospital to see Gino. Since yesterday, when he was admitted, Blade has been trying to find the fucker who shot him, but until a few minutes ago, he still has had no luck. Gino is now in the ICU, fighting for his life. The doctors still don't know if he will make it. The men are all up in arms, wanting to make someone pay, and someone will pay, but we need to make sure we get the right person and don't go out on a killing spree and kill innocent people.

"They will, Vito," I say as I step out of the car to make my way inside. At the door, Antonio inclines his head inside, indicating there is someone to see me. I walk in to see Alfredo sitting at one of the tables. Sitting before him is a woman. I can't see her face, as her back is to me, but going by the colour and length of her hair, I would say it's his daughter. I really don't have time for this today, as I have a meeting with the head of the Ukrainians in an hour.

As soon as Alfredo sees me, he is on his feet. His daughter continues sitting, a sign that she doesn't want to be here. "Alfredo," I greet, purposefully standing behind his daughter, waiting for her to acknowledge me.

"I have my daughter, Lola, with me." He points to her. "You said you wanted to meet her before agreeing." His daughter finally turns in her seat to look at me. The first thing that pops into my mind is that she is more beautiful in person than in the photo, and by her set features, I would say that she is not happy at this solution.

"Lola, are you okay with this?" I see her surprise at my question.

"Not really, but doesn't seem like we have a choice."

"This is not your debt; it is your father's debt. You have a choice," I say, only to see her shake her beautiful head, her hair glistening as the overhead lights shine down on her.

"He is my father; therefore, his debt is also mine."

Well, it looks like the daughter has higher standards than the dad does. "What do you do now?"

She shrugs as she stands and finally turns towards me fully. She is a petite little thing, wearing tight black jeans and a red T-shirt that says "Don't touch this," her perky breasts hidden under it.

"I work at a diner across town from seven in the morning until after lunch, and then I have college from two thirty until eight at night every day of the week."

So, she is a hard worker, and it looks like she counts on her work instead of luck, unlike her father. "What are you studying?"

"Accounting."

I'm surprised at her answer, as she doesn't look like any accountant I have seen before. "What do you do on the weekends?"

"I worked at the diner this morning, and usually I work on assignments during the rest of the weekend."

"Okay, give Antonio your number. Someone will contact you to agree on conditions." I step around her to make my way to my office, and then stop. "Alfredo." I turn to look at him. "You are a lucky man to have a daughter like her who values *familia*. It is time you start showing her that you appreciate it." I don't wait for a reply, but turn and make my way to the back. I will get Blade to arrange her a job, but for now, I have other things to think about, like the Ukrainian meeting.

"Where's Joey?" I ask as I walk towards my desk.

"I'm here," Joey says as he walks in, followed by Blade.

"Did you find him?" I ask, looking at Blade, only to see him shaking his head.

"The fucker is hiding," Vito mutters as he takes a seat on the couch.

"For the meeting, I only want Viktor and one of his men in here. Joey, you and Vito stay with any other men he brings in front. Blade, you join us here." There is a knock on the door, and Antonio sticks his head around the door.

"They're here, Boss," he states before closing the door again.

"You two go. Blade, you walk them in." All three leave as I take my seat behind my mahogany desk. My hand strokes the gun I have on the inside of my desk. All I have to do is slide it out of the holster and shoot. I have one on each side for good measure. In this line of business, you can never be too safe. Blade opens the door to the office. Standing back, he lets Viktor and his man enter. Viktor is a tall, heavy-set man with thinning black hair and a scar down his neck that looks like someone tried to kill him but clearly missed.

"Dom," Viktor greets as he takes a seat on one of the chairs before me. His man lounges on the couch to the side.

"Viktor, thank you for coming," I say, leaning back on my chair. We are both summing each other up, trying to find weaknesses.

"You called. I was curious," he says in his thick accent.

"You have been selling your product in my streets. You know I don't want drugs on my turf."

He shrugs casually. "It was just a few bags. You want commission?" He lifts his hand and clicks his fingers. His man on the couch pulls out a pack of cigarettes and proceeds to light one. He then stands and brings it over to Viktor.

"I don't want commission from your sales, Viktor. I don't want the product on my streets."

He blows out a puff of smoke as he sits forward. "We have a problem, yes, as I have clients on your streets." He smiles, but his smile doesn't reach his dead and unfeeling eyes.

"Well, then you will have to tell your clients to go to your side and purchase your merchandise."

Viktor starts shaking his head in denial. "Naa, I don't think that will work for us," he says with a shrug.

"If we find anyone selling on our streets, they will be killed." If that is the route I have to take to keep my people free of drugs, then that is what I will do.

Viktor shrugs, and his lips kick up on one side. "Are you sure you want to do that? I believe you already have one man in the hospital."

I tense at his provocative comment. "And when we find the man who shot him, he will be dead."

Viktor shrugs as he stands. He brings his cigarette down on my desk, putting it out on the shiny wood. Son of a bitch is provoking me, but I don't lose my cool as easily as he might expect. He will pay for that; I will burn his laundry shop, where he has his office, to the ground.

"He is just another man," he says as he turns to leave.

"Viktor," I call before he reaches the door. "This is war." He throws back his head and laughs. The son of a bitch thinks this is funny. Well, he won't be laughing once he deals with the Capella family. We might try to keep the peace whenever we can, but we do not run from a fight, and when we are provoked into a fight, we will die before we let our family be hurt.

"I want to slit his fucking throat," Blade says when they are both gone. He approaches the desk to look down at the mark of the cigarette.

"Get someone to sort that out," I mutter as Vito and Joey walk in. Vito looks at the desk and frowns, but then walks out again.

"What happened?" Joey asks as he also looks at the desk.

"When Vito comes back, we will discuss it." Joey looks from me to Blade and then back towards me before he nods and takes a seat on the same chair where Viktor sat. Vito comes in a couple minutes later, pocketing his phone.

"He will be here within the hour to polish the desk," Vito says as he sits on the chair next to Joey. "So, what did I miss?"

"We are at war with the Ukrainians," I state, "because they shot Gino, as my third Capo, I will have Blade here as the underboss he will see to Gino's men until he is back in post or until we find someone to take his place."

"Fuck," Joey mutters.

"I want you to meet with your soldiers. You tell them that we are at war. From now on, anyone caught selling on our streets is killed—not wounded, killed. I want everyone warned, right down to our associates. If anyone sees anything, they are to report it to us. We are to keep everyone as safe as possible. They are trying to infiltrate their drugs into our community. We will not let them."

"I will speak to the cleaner for him to be ready," Vito says. The cleaner is one of our men who makes anyone we don't want found disappear.

"Joey, I need you to speak to our contact and get as much ammunition as he can get. I want all our men armed at all times." Joey nods, waiting for me to finish. "Blade, are you okay with standing in for Gino for a while?" Blade nods. "Good, see what information you can get from your dad about the Ukrainians, and we are going to need eyes on their territory."

"What can we expect from them?" Vito asks as he rubs at his stubble.

"You can expect what you got with Gino. They are crafty. Always be on your guard. From today, I don't want anyone alone. They will always be in pairs." They grunt their agreements. "Any more questions?" I look around at each one before dismissing them to go do what I ordered.

On the way out, Blade stops. "Antonio gave me this piece of paper with a number. He said you would tell me about it." I frown at first, not understanding, and then the image of Lola pops into my mind.

"That is the number for Alfredo's daughter. Get her a job waitressing somewhere, or at a till. She is studying accounting, so she needs time to study. Organize with her, and we get fifty percent of her wages to pay towards Alfredo's debt." Blade frowns but doesn't comment as he nods and leaves.

This is the worst time to work for the Capella family, but an agreement is an agreement, and we protect those who work for us. Viktor thinks that he can just encroach on our territory and we will just stand by and let him. Well, he will find out who we are and what we are made of and will never again take others for granted.

I know that we will have fatalities and wins, but what matters is that at the end of this war, our *familia* is safe and that our kids will grow up without us worrying about addictions. My phone starts to ring. Grunting, I pull it out of my jacket pocket to see that it's the hospital. My stomach tightens. Is this going to be bad news? Are they going to tell me that Gino is dead?

"Yes?"

"Is this Mr. Capella?"

"Yes."

"I am phoning from St. Mary's Hospital to let you know that Mr. Ricci is awake."

I sigh in relief. "Is he fine?"

"He isn't out of the woods yet, but he is now conscious, which is a good sign."

"Thank you." It is a relief to know that Gino is going to pull through, and the man who shot him will be found and killed. I have a man with Gino at all times, but I think I will get someone else there, too, as I didn't like Viktor knowing that Gino is in the hospital and still alive.

Today might mark the beginning of the day the war begins with the Ukrainians, but when I think of what the Capella family is about, doing all that is needed for the family, protecting and standing by them no matter what, an image of Lola pops to mind, which has me frowning. She surprised me today with her dedication to her father. Not only is she beautiful, but she is a rare gem. It is a shame that she has a father like she does who will give her heartache throughout her life.

LOLA 4

It has been a week since the day I first met Dom Capella. I thought they had forgotten about the deal we made, but this morning, I received a call from someone called Tina. To my surprise, I was asked when the best times were for me to work, and an agreement was reached that I'm happy with. This week has been hell. I've been doing my head in wondering what kind of conditions and job I would have to do. The pay is also more than what I am getting at the diner. Even with the fifty-percent deduction every month that will go towards Papa's debt, I will still be getting just over what I was getting at the diner.

The only difference is that now instead of working in the morning and studying in the evenings, I am studying in the mornings and will be working in the evenings from seven to one, three times a week and every weekend, as it is a club and apparently really busy on weekends. When I told Dina where I was going to be working, she was beyond herself, raving about how difficult it is to get in, as it's one of the most popular clubs in the city now.

Taking in a deep breath, I walk up to the guy leaning against the side door and smoking a cigarette. His eyes follow me suspiciously. "Hi, I'm here to start working today," I say, and he raises a brow.

"No one told me that we had someone new today," he says with a shrug.

Great. If they made me waste my time coming in today, I am not going to be happy. "I spoke to Tina on the phone. She said I should be here at this time to fill in some papers."

He takes another puff of his cigarette before he nods and stands up straight away from the wall he was leaning against. Pulling out his phone, he dials. A minute later, he turns around and talks to whomever he dialled.

"What's your name?" he asks as he pockets the phone.

"Lola."

He nods as he opens the door. "Lola, go down the corridor to the last door. You will find Tina behind the bar. She will take you from there."

"Thanks," I say as I step past him to enter the building.

"And, Lola." I look back over my shoulder at him. "Welcome to Club Olympus. If anyone gives you any trouble, just speak to me."

"Thank you." Only when I'm at the end of the corridor do I realize that I didn't ask him what his name was. Oh well, I'm sure I will find out soon enough. Opening the door to the club, I stop and look around. There are two girls talking by one of the tables, and three leaning against the counter, talking. When I walk in, the girls by the main counter stop talking and look at me.

"You must be Lola." I jump in surprise. Looking behind me, I see a woman who must be in her late twenties looking at me. Her eyes sum me up as she looks over my body. "I have the contract in the office. Follow me." Well, she's not very friendly, is she? I turn and follow her down the way I came until she stops before she opens a door and enters. Walking to the desk, she lifts a piece of paper and hands it to me. "This has everything we spoke about on the phone. Don't think that because you have a contract, you don't have to work. Here, if you don't pull your weight, you get kicked out, and then we know what will happen, don't we?"

I hate the way she thinks that she can hold my situation over my head. "I am here to work. I don't plan on giving you any problems."

She frowns at me before she nods, handing me a pen. "Sign, and then I will show you where you can leave your stuff. You will be serving at the tables tonight; you will find three T-shirts in your locker." She looks over my body again. "I'm sure they will fit you; I expect you to wear the club shirt when you're here, and they are to be clean at all times." I glance down at the piece of paper and see that it's a simple contract with my name and the conditions stipulated on it, the salary is at the bottom as discussed. I lean over, placing the contract on the desk, and sign under my name.

"Do I get a copy?"

She raises a thin brow at me as I place the pen on top of the piece of paper. "As soon as it gets signed, I will give you a copy." I guess it's not her signing, then. "Now come, I will show you where the changing room is where you can change into one of the shirts, and then one of the other girls will show you around." I follow her out of the office and across the corridor to another door that she opens to show the changing room. Stepping inside after her, I see that the changing room is neat and nothing is out of place. Everything is spotless.

"Here, this one is yours," Tina says as she stops in front of a locker, lifting her hand to show a set of keys. "These are your locker keys; we have never had any stealing here, but I'd rather be safe than sorry." I take the keys from her hand. "I will send one of the girls to come get you." And with those words, she turns and leaves me standing here, looking around.

Well, it looks like this is going to be my workplace for a few years, because there is no way I can pay the Capella family off sooner on my salary, but I am hoping that after I finish my course, I can find myself a day job that will pay me a decent salary, and then I can start paying more into this debt. Opening my locker, I see the three shirts inside. Pulling out the T-shirt, I sigh. Lifting it up before me, I wrinkle my nose. The ocean-blue shirt will be skin tight and end just under my breasts. It's not the most revealing T-shirt I have seen, but it's also not normal day-to-day wear.

"Oh, well." Shrugging, I stuff my haversack in the locker and then pull off the black T-shirt I am wearing. Folding it, I place it inside the locker before sliding the blue one on. I pull at it until I'm relatively happy that it's covering as much as it will. I pull my hair loose from inside the shirt and adjust my ponytail. Well, I'm as ready as I'm ever going to be. I am just sliding the keys for the locker into my front pocket of my black body-fitting jeans when the door to the locker room opens and in walks one of the girls I saw standing by the counter.

"Hi, I'm Debbie. I'm here to show you around and teach you the ropes." Debbie seems friendly, which is a relief after dealing with Tina.

"Hi, Debbie, nice to meet you."

"Well, let's show you around before the rush begins," she says as she opens the door. "I will introduce you to everyone, but don't worry if you don't remember names. It took me forever before I remembered everyone." Debbie guides me around the club, introducing me to the other employees and all the different sections. When we come to the third floor and apparently the VIP lounge, I am surprised at how big the club is.

I understand why Olympus is one of the best clubs in town. Apparently no cost was spared when it came to the interior of the club, and it looks like it paid off, as Debbie says that the club is full nearly every night, and on Fridays and Saturdays, people stand in line to get in.

"So where will I be working?" I ask as Debbie starts leading me downstairs again.

"Well, the roster is downstairs by the door to the changing room, but today, you will be taking orders in the south section downstairs with me so you can get the hang of things." I'm happy with that, as I must be honest—the only job that I have had is at the diner serving tables. "If you have any problems with any of the customers, just call

Tommy. You must have met him when you walked in, or there are always Capella men hanging around."

I turn my head as I hear a bell. "Well, things are about to start getting exciting. Are you ready?" Debbie has been nothing but sweet and helpful, and I think I will enjoy getting to know her.

"I guess we will find out," I say as I see people starting to make their way inside. From that minute on, there isn't a spare minute to think about anything except work. By the end of the evening, I am so tired, I could sleep standing up. I really need to get used to this rhythm, and quickly, or I'm going to struggle to keep up.

By the time I make my way to the changing room, it's nearly one thirty in the morning. I have never been on the tube so late at night, but it will have to be, as it's the only way I'm going to get home at this time without my own transport. Changing into my own T-shirt, I look up as Debbie and another girl Chloe walk in. "So how was it?" Chloe asks as she walks towards her locker.

"I'm dead," I confess, only to hear both of them laugh in amusement.

"Don't worry, you'll get used to it, you'll see," Debbie says as she holds out an envelope towards me. "Here's your cut."

I look at the envelope and frown. "What is that?"

"Our tips. At the end of the night, it gets split between all of us." I take the envelope, surprised, as I didn't think we would be getting any tips. Every extra change counts. I won't turn it down, that's for sure.

"Thank you," I say as I pocket the envelope in my front jean pocket. "Well, I better go, or I'll never get home." I pull the haversack over my shoulder.

"How are you getting home?" Chloe asks as she slides on her jacket before picking up her handbag.

"Oh, I'm catching the tube." I make my way towards the door. "Bye," I call as I slip out. I walk down the corridor and am nearly at the outside door when a door to my left opens. Looking inside as I pass, I see Dom behind a desk, a man standing next to him, and another one at the door about to walk out. I see Dom looking up as I walk past, but I'm not sure if he sees me.

"Well, hello there." My hand is on the handle, about to open the outside door, when I hear the voice behind me. I snap around in surprise to see the man who was walking out of the office right behind me. "And who might you be? I've never seen you here before."

"Joey." I look behind him to see Dom standing at the door to his office. The man looks over his shoulder at Dom. "No."

The man tenses. "Oh, come on." Dom raises his brow but doesn't say anything else to Joey. "Fine, see you tomorrow." Joey places his hand over mine, opens the door, and then steps around me and leaves. Did he just warn him off me?

"How are you getting home?" Dom suddenly asks as I turn to follow Joey. I stop and look back at him.

"I'm catching the tube," I say, turning again to leave. I walk all the way around the club and am about to cross the street, when a big black car stops before me. I see Tommy in the driver's seat. He pulls down his window and then tells me to get in.

"It's fine, thank you. I'm just going down the street."

"Stop being stubborn and get in." I place my hands on my hips and frown at him.

"Don't take this the wrong way, but I don't really know you."

He shakes his head in annoyance. "Look, I also want to get to bed, okay? Now get in the car because the sooner I get you home, the sooner I can get home."

"I'm not getting in the car with you." There is no way I am getting in a car with a total stranger, and even though I know he works here, it is the first time I have met him. I turn to walk around the car, when he parks and opens his door.

"Look, the boss wants you home safe. Now, will you get in the fucking car, or must I make you?" At his words, I tense. Dom told him to take me home. Well, he will have to be disappointed, because I agreed to work for him to pay off my debt. I didn't agree to do anything else.

"Well, you can tell your boss that I can make it home on my own. I don't need a bodyguard." No sooner are the words out of my mouth then he is headed towards me. "What are you doing?" I ask in surprise; I turn and am about to start running, when he places his hands around my waist and lifts me over his shoulder.

"Now stop being so fucking stubborn. The boss said you get home safe, and that is what is going to happen."

"Tommy." The snap of that voice has him stopping in his tracks. My hair is hanging in my eyes, so I can't see anything, but I can imagine how it looks with me over this lug's shoulder with my bum up in the air.

"She didn't want to get into the car."

"Put her down." I immediately feel myself sliding down until my feet are touching the ground. Huffing in annoyance, I turn around to see Dom standing at the curb, another car idling behind Tommy's. The man who was standing next to Dom when I walked past the door to the office is behind the wheel, looking at us.

"What is the problem?" Dom asks, looking at me.

"This was not part of the contract; I can find my own way home." He frowns, his eyes sparkling in anger. I don't think Mr. Dom Capella is used to anyone contradicting him.

"You either get in the car right now, or the contract is null and void and the debt will be up for collection immediately. I will not be responsible if anything happens to you." I gasp at his statement; how dare he change the rules to suite him. I can see that he means every word he is saying, so without a word, I make my way towards the passenger side of Tommy's car. "No, that one." I stop to see him inclining his head to the car idling behind Tommy's.

I lift my head in anger but make my way towards the car. Opening the back door, I slide in. I see Dom saying something to Tommy, and then he walks towards the car. Damn, man thinks just because he's the head of the Capella family, he can tell me what to do. Well, I won't let him.

DOM 5

As I slide into the car, I see the glance Blade gives me. He must be wondering why I would care if the fool girl wants to get herself killed. "Where to?" Blade asks, looking in the rear-view mirror. Lola mentions the address. I can hear the reluctance in her voice, but she knows that it's no use fighting against me.

As we pull away from the curb, I see the car parked at the end of the street. As we approach, there are two men sitting inside, and they look at us as we pass. "See them?" Blade asks.

"Yeah." Viktor has his men staking out the place. We have now seen his men in various locations. He is trying to unsettle us. Well, he will have to try harder. "Tommy will be taking you home every night when you finish." I hear a huff from behind.

"Thank you for the concern, but I have managed to keep safe until now. I'm sure I will be fine going forward." I lean my head back and close my eyes, sighing. It has been a long day. I would think that the last thing I would feel like doing is dealing with a firecracker like her, but I can feel the excitement that builds at her rebellious nature.

"There will be no discussion on this. Tommy lives near you. He will drop you off after work. If he isn't available, another of our men will do it, but you will not travel alone." I hear her exaggerated sigh and feel my lips twitching. "You are part of the Capella family, now and we make sure that everyone under us is safe."

"Look, I am not a part of anything. The only thing I'm doing is working off the debt. Besides that, I'm not interested. I thank you for allowing us to pay the debt off like this, but that's all it is." I hear a grunt. Looking towards Blade, I see him grinning. I'm sure he's enjoying this. The only person who gives me shit is him.

"As I said, there will be no discussion." She must have done something, because suddenly, I hear Blade chuckling as he looks into the rear-view mirror.

"Maybe I'll start taking her home. She's amusing," he says as he winks in the rear-view mirror.

I glance over at him and scowl. "You have other stuff to do." And if he doesn't, I will find him something to do.

"I'm sure I could make time for a sweet little thing like her." I'm about to tell him to shut it, when Lola interrupts me.

"I'm right here," she mutters, and I can just imagine her glaring at both of us. Blade turns up a side street and then stops. I look up the darkened street to make sure that there is no one lurking in the darkness. Opening my door, I step out to find her already stepping out the back and closing the door behind her.

"Is your dad home?" I ask, looking up at the darkened house.

"Yes, he'll be sleeping. Thank you," she mutters as she turns to make her way inside, her round bottom catching my eye. Fuck, she's a sexy little thing. I can feel myself hardening as I see her swinging her hips as she makes her way to the front door. She doesn't look back as she enters and closes the door behind her.

As I slide into the car, I can see Blade's amused glance. "Since when did we start taking employees home to keep them safe?"

"Since we are at war and she's travelling at two in the morning. I would rather her not get shot because she's trying to pay for her father's debt."

"Sure it is," he says with a grin. "I have never seen you go to so much trouble for a woman before. It will be interesting."

"There is nothing interesting, just what I told you," I state as I lean back.

"Sure, that's why I thought you were about to shoot Tommy when we came out of the car park and you saw her over his shoulder." I must be honest—I didn't like seeing his hands on her. The thought still has my anger rising, but I understand that he was trying to follow my orders. As we turn down a side street that will lead us towards my home, I see Blade looking in his rear-view mirror.

Looking out the side mirror, I see headlights approaching. "They've been following us," Blade says as he accelerates.

"You sure it's them?" I ask.

"Yeah." I pull out my phone and dial Vito. A minute later, he answers. By the quiet in the background, I would say he's already at home.

"Boss?"

"Vito, are you home?"

"Yes."

"Blade and I are headed home. Viktor's men are following us. We're going to drive past your house. When they come, tell your men to shoot them." We have guards at all our homes just to make sure there are no surprises during the night. These fuckers will learn not to follow us.

"On it," he says as he disconnects.

"I bet you Vito will be there with his men shooting," Blade says. We both know that when it comes to shootouts, Vito is the first one there. He leads by example; he will never tell his men to do something if he isn't willing to do it with them. We are about two minutes away from Vito's property. As we speed towards it, I can see two cars parked on the road, one on each side. They seem deserted, but I know that the men are there waiting.

As soon as we pass, I see the men. There are two on each side, and then I see Vito duck behind the pillar at the entrance to his driveway. "Yeah, there he is. Was he naked?" Blade asks with a laugh.

"No, I'm sure I saw boxers." We hear shots and then a crash. "Turn around." A few minutes later, we are pulling up next to the car that was following us. Vito's top half is in through the driver's window, and he is punching. The guy on the passenger side seems to be dead.

"Boss," the men greet as I approach.

"Vito, enough." The guy seems to be dead already. He pulls back, turning towards me. "You know what to do." He nods. I know that soon, the cleaner will be called, and the bodies will disappear, never to be found again. The car will be taken to the scrap yard and destroyed together with anything else they might find in it. I look around to see if there might be anyone out, but the houses down this road all belong to the Capella family; therefore, we are certain no one will call the cops on us.

"Nice work," I call as I make my way back to the car. Just before I get in, I turn around. "Hey, Vito, nice boxers." The men all start to chuckle as they look at his boxers. In the front, they have an image of hands ripping material and the words "careful with the beast" printed over his crotch. I see him looking down and then grinning. Trust him to wear something like that.

"I think I'm going to get Vito to get you a pair of those." I look at him, raising a brow. "But it will have to say 'the real boss.'" I grin at his joke, shaking my head in amusement.

"Wonder what yours would say," I mutter.

"All-powerful," he jokes, which has me grinning.

"Maybe we should get Mr. All-Powerful to fight the Ukrainians, then."

"Those assholes, you should just let me go there and slit their fucking throats while they sleep," Blade mutters as he turns into my driveway. He drives up to the house. Stopping, he turns off the car. "I think there is someone slipping them information."

"What do you know?" One thing I will never accept is someone who turns on family. If anyone betrays us, they are dead.

"Twice they have known where we are going to be, and one pair of eyes that I had placed in their territory was killed yesterday.

"Do you have any idea who it could be?" Blade raises his hands, rubbing his face before looking at me.

"Where we were going to be a few people could have known. For that information, I will have to look into it, but the eyes I placed in their territory only Joey, Vito, you, and me knew about."

I frown. "I trust Joey and Vito; they would never betray the *familia*."

"I know. That is why we are going to have your office at the club swept for bugs first thing in the morning." I know that all the places we frequent are swept for bugs once a month, but if there is a listening device in my office, that means someone at the club has gone in there and planted it. That could only be one of the employees or one of our men.

"If you do find any, then we have a problem." Only a very few are allowed into my office. Those few are trusted employees who have been with the club for a long time. If there are listening devices in the office, then it means that one of them betrayed us. We treat our people fairly, protecting them from everything and helping them when we can. We have always been open to helping those who find themselves in a tight spot; that's why we have never had problems before of anyone betraying us.

"There must be another explanation. I can't believe any of our people would do that." Blade nods at my comment, but I can see the suspicion on his face. "Why don't you stay here tonight? You can go home tomorrow." Blade stays in one of the spare rooms sometimes when it gets late or when we have things to deal with early in the morning.

"Naa, it's okay. I need to go see if my place is still in the same place and make sure there is no one lurking in my bed." At his comment, I laugh, as I remember a few years ago one of his conquests decided to break in and make herself at home in his bed. When he came home with another woman, to his surprise, she was lying there naked, waiting for him.

"Okay, see you tomorrow." I get out of the car, making my way inside. As I approach the door, Alberto opens it for me. Alberto has been with me since I was a baby. He used to be my personal guard, and then with time, he was promoted to securing all the Capella bosses' private residences. No matter how late it is, Alberto is always here, ready to welcome me. When my father passed and the others stepped down, I kept Alberto in his post, as he has no one else except the *familia*.

"Alberto."

"Boss," he greets. No matter how many times I have told him to call me Dom, he insists on calling me boss, as he says it would be disrespectful of him.

"What are you still doing up? I saw the men patrolling the grounds. You should be in bed by now."

"When we are at war, we sleep with one eye open," he says. "We are always ready for problems." Alberto is old school. I used to spend a lot of hours with Alberto growing up, listening to his stories. Sometimes when I'm struggling with a decision, he is the one I speak to when I need to know what my father would do.

"Well, I'm off to bed. You should do the same," I say as I tap him on the back as I walk past.

"You need a good woman to come home to. That makes all the difference, gives you a reason to fight." An image of Lola fills my mind, and instantly, I can feel my body reacting. What about her has triggered my interest? I have been with many beautiful women; why her? I think it's the values that she holds about *familia* that has tweaked my interest, but whatever it is, it's clearly not reciprocated, as she doesn't even seem to like me as a person.

"Women just bring you headaches," I say as I start making my way upstairs.

"No, the right woman makes everything better." I know that Alberto was married for a very short time in his young years, but his wife died in childbirth together with their son. He never took another woman to wed after her, and swears that the right woman makes a man better.

"You are becoming soft in your old years," I tease. "Goodnight." I walk down the corridor to the master bedroom, pulling off my jacket. It has been a long night; Viktor has his men trying to infiltrate our streets, but the Capella family has unity on our side, which he will never have. The people who live and work in my streets have all come together to fight this threat that is trying to disrupt our lives. I think back to Lola and grunt as I remember her feisty attitude as she tried to stand up to me.

She has the heart of a fighter and the beauty of a siren. I will do well to keep away from that one.

LOLA 6

"What happened?" I ask as I walk up to Tommy. In the last two weeks since my first day here at Olympus, Tommy and I have become friends. Every night, he will wait for me before taking me home. In those two weeks, I haven't spoken to Dom again, but sometimes, I have felt eyes on me while working. When turning, I have caught his eyes on me. I will confess only to myself that he is a magnetic and handsome man, but he is dangerous.

When I leave for the night, I always see him in his office. Sometimes he has men in there; sometimes he is by himself. I keep my eyes forward and make sure not to engage in conversation with him. I have also heard rumours that Tina has staked a claim on him, and she can become mean when contradicted, as I have realized in these last two weeks that I have worked here.

One thing that I have also realized is that there is some kind of scheming going on around the club, as I have noticed that not all the orders get registered. Now I don't know if that is on purpose to hide profits, or if Julian, who usually works till, is just pocketing cash, but whatever it is, it has been happening since I started. I can't believe Tina wouldn't realize the discrepancy by now, so it brings me to believe that it is a decision from management.

Either way, I keep my head down and don't make waves, as I am only here for one reason and one reason only, but to be honest, this place is starting to grow on me. Debbie and Chloe are great, and we have many laughs together.

"There was a shooting earlier, a drive-by." Tommy says, I look at the police as they close off the area with their yellow tape.

"Was anyone hurt?"

"Julian was shot. He was rushed to the hospital, and a guy who was walking past died." My heart is racing at the news. I don't know Julian that well, but we have spoken sometimes. He must be in his late twenties, and even though just a minute ago I was thinking that he must be stealing from the club, I would never want him any harm. "You better get inside. These days it's not safe outside anymore."

I got Dina on the list to come to the club tonight, as she has been bugging me ever since I got this job, but now I feel like phoning her and telling her not to come, but knowing Dina, she won't care about the danger and will want to come anyway.

I am just about to step inside, when I see three cars driving up to the club. The windows are tinted, but I know that Dom will be in one of them. "Get inside," Tommy states as he walks towards the cars. I hurry inside, making my way towards the changing room, only to find five of the girls there talking about the shooting. Two are crying at Julian being shot, and the others are standing around talking.

"Hi."

"Have you heard what happened?" one of the girls asks.

"Yes, I've just heard," I say as I walk towards my locker to lock away my haversack. Today, I already have my Olympus T-shirt on under my hoodie. Pulling the hoodie off, I hang it on the hanger before closing my locker while I listen to the girls talking.

"Everyone in front," Tina calls from the doorway. Looking over, I see her standing there with her usual frown. I don't know what it is, but she doesn't like me. Every time she looks at me, she glares. Debbie says I shouldn't worry about it, as she will come around, but it's been two weeks and I'm still getting the cold shoulder.

I follow her down the corridor to the front to find the other staff standing there waiting. Looks like we are having a meeting, but it's only natural with what has just happened. "Settle down," Tina calls as she goes to stand before the group. "I'm sure you have all heard what happened earlier today." There are comments, but they die down when she raises one of her hands in silence. "The cops will be talking to some of you later. They have been told to do it before we open. It will be business as usual. I will be taking Julian's place for now."

"Lola will." My eyes snap to the door that leads to the corridor, only now noticing Dom and Blade standing there. What the hell does he mean I will?

"She has no experience with the till," Tina says with a scowl.

"I'm sure she will be fine," he says as he walks towards her. Coming to stand next to her, he stops, facing everyone. "I've just heard from the hospital; Julian was shot in his side, and luckily the bullet missed all major organs, which means that he will soon be fine. I want you all to be vigilant. If you see anything out of the ordinary, be it here or outside, you let us know. I want you all to know that we have upped the security. We will keep you safe."

After a few questions from the staff are answered, he turns, heading back towards his office. I see him saying something to one of his men, who nods. Tina hurries after him, no doubt to ask him why he wants me at the till.

"Well, looks like you won't be with us for a while," Chloe says as she walks past.

"You know Tina is not going to like that, don't you?" Debbie says as we make our way towards the counter to get the cleaning supplies, only to be stopped by the man I saw Dom talk to.

"Come with me."

"Good luck," Debbie calls as I follow him. Great, I feel like I've been called to the principal's office.

"Wait here," he says as he knocks on the door. He then opens it and sticks his head around. "She's here."

"This isn't right," I hear Tina say in an angry voice before the door opens and she walks out, not even glancing at me. The guy who brought me here inclines his head for me to enter. Taking a deep breath, I walk in, hearing the door close behind me. I see Dom sitting behind his desk, a file open before him. As I approach, he looks up at me, his eyes travelling over my body. His dark-brown eyes smoulder with heat as they take in every inch of my body, my stomach knotting with excitement.

What is it about him that has my heart racing every time I see him? His very presence has me in a tailspin.

"Lola, take a seat." He points towards the chairs before his desk as he looks back down at the file on his desk to close it. I walk towards one of the chairs. Sitting, I wait. He finally looks back up at me and then stands and walks around his desk. He comes to stand between the desk and my chair. Leaning against the desk, he looks down at me, making me uncomfortable.

"Why do you want me at the till?" I ask before he can speak.

"You have worked at the diner, and you are nearly finished with your accounting training. You're the best person for the job." He crosses his ankles, which has his leg touching mine. My reaction is to move my legs away, but I still that telltale sign of weakness.

"I've only been here for two weeks; I doubt I'm the best person for the position." He raises a brow, which makes the scar on his forehead more pronounced. Not for the first time, I wonder what happened to give him that scar.

"Do you think you can't do it?"

My eyes snap back to his. "I didn't say that."

"Then what are you saying?" he asks, crossing his arms over his chest, the fabric of his light-grey shirt stretching over its breadth.

"Just that it might cause problems."

"Let me worry about that."

"So why exactly did you call me in here?" I ask with a frown.

"I wanted to know how these last two weeks have been. Looks like you integrated right in from what I've seen."

"It's good, thank you." I jump up from my seat. "If that is all you wanted, I'll be getting back to work." The longer I sit here looking at him, the more nervous I get. I feel his hand clasp my upper arm as I start to turn, and then I am being pulled up against his chest. His scent engulfs me as his other arm snakes around my waist.

"What are you doi—" Before I can finish my sentence, his lips are over mine and he is kissing the breath out of me. My hands come up; I start to push him away, but the arm he has around my waist tightens, pulling me more firmly against him. Damn, how can he kiss so well? All I know is that one minute I am fighting him, and then next, my arms are around his shoulders, my fingers entwined in his dark-brown hair. The hand that was holding my upper arm has slid down to my naked navel. I can feel the warmth of his fingers as he strokes my skin.

His lips are relentless. All I can think about is how hot this man is making me; I can feel his hardness poking into me. The arm at my waist has slid down, his hand grabbing my ass at the same time as his other hand on my navel rises under the Olympus shirt to stroke the nipple covered with a silky white bra. The friction of the movement over my pebbled nipple makes me sigh in pleasure.

Suddenly, he lifts his head. The hand at my breast descends to join his other one at my ass. He lifts me. Turning, he places me on the desk. I hear something crash to the floor, but I don't look, as I see his passion-filled eyes looking at me. "I want you," he mutters, and then his hands are on my T-shirt and he is pulling it off.

What am I doing? I can't do this; he is the Capella family boss, and I am not a back-office kind of girl. His hands are pulling my bra away from my breasts, his head lowering. "Wait," I gasp, my hands rising towards his shoulders. "No, wait," I murmur again as his lips close over one of my nipples. He raises his head, his eyes focusing on me. Oh, why is he so damn handsome?

"I can't do this."

"Why? Are you in a relationship?"

I shake my head at his question. "What? No."

His eyebrow rises in question as he slowly stands up straight, but I notice that his hands are still firmly on my body. "So, what's the problem?"

"You're my boss, and I'm not that type of girl."

"I know you are not that type of girl," he states, a serious note in his tone. "You want me to fire you? Because, Lola, you and I both know that we have wanted this since the day we met."

"Is this why you had me placed at the till?" I will not work till if he thinks he is buying himself favours.

"No, I want you at the till because I think you are capable of doing that job and because I am tired of seeing the customers ogling over you. If another one touches you inappropriately, he will lose his fucking hands." I gasp. I never realized that he knew about that. Two days ago, while I was taking an order, one of the customers, a guy in his late thirties, decided he had free access to my ass. I stepped away and put him in his place, but in his defence, he was drunk, so I doubt he even heard me above the music at the club. He was stretching out for me again, when one of Dom's men stepped in and escorted him outside.

"Is this part of the new job description?"

He frowns. "No, this is part of what has been between us from the beginning."

I place my hands over his, pulling them away from my body as I slip off the desk. "I need to get back to work," I mutter. I can feel the heat on my cheeks as I adjust the bra over my breasts and then pull my T-shirt down, covering myself as much as it will allow.

"This isn't finished," he warns as I walk past, but at the door, I stop and turn to find his eyes on me.

"Am I supposed to do what Julian was doing? Because I'll tell you now I don't agree with that."

He frowns. "What do you mean?" His voice is a gravely masculine timbre that makes bumps rise on my skin.

"Not registering all the orders, because if you are doing it to trick the tax man, you forgot you're purchasing invoices. They will catch you like that." I see a transformation come over him. His features tense, and his body isn't as relaxed as before. I realize that maybe I shouldn't have said anything, but I refuse to do his dirty work.

"No, I want everything by the book." Before I can say anything else, the door opens, just missing me as I quickly jump out of the way.

"Sorry, didn't know you had company," Blade says as he steps inside.

"It's okay. I have to get back to work. Excuse me." I leave before Dom or Blade can say anything else. My heart is racing as I realize that if it were a few minutes earlier, Blade would have caught the two of us. Hurrying towards my new workstation to familiarize myself with the till, I grunt when I see cops talking to some of the girls. Today has been different. My heart is still racing at Dom's kiss, and my stomach is knotted in frustration. It would have been so easy to let him have his way with me. He is right about one thing—I have been fascinated with him since the moment I first saw him.

I see Blade look down at the ground next to my desk where the lamp lies shattered, a grin lifting his lips. "Did I interrupt something?" he asks.

"Close the door," I mutter. I am not in the mood to joke around. I walk around my desk. Taking a seat, I look at Blade as he walks towards me.

"I want Jameson and his team here as soon as possible; I want a deep dive into the club's accounts." Blade's expression changes at my request. A frown adorns his features as he takes a seat before me.

"Anything I should know?" he asks.

"Lola just said something that, if correct, means we have a problem." Fuck, just saying her name has me wanting to follow her and show her who's boss.

"I will have him here tomorrow morning," Blade confirms.

"Make sure that no one goes near any of the accounts from now until he is finished." If what Lola says is correct, we have a thief among us. It's not just about being a thief, but the fact that it will place the Capella family at risk of tax evasion. "I want to speak to him before he starts, and I want you here so you know what is going on."

"I hate everything to do with fucking accounts," Blade mutters. "Seeing we're on the subject of money, the crack house they set up has been burnt down. There won't be any more moneymaking for them through there." One of our soldiers heard that Viktor had set up shop right under our noses. We have now shut the shop down. The fucker has been true to his nature, sneaking his drugs in every chance he gets.

With the one today, there has been three shootings since the war started, with two deaths from our side. We have attacked them in different ways. Three of their men have been found selling on our streets, and they have been killed. The two who were following us were also killed. We shut down their crack house and have some of their operations in their territory under surveillance.

"Have you found any leads on who placed the bugs in my office?" When the office was checked, four devices were found. That has me fucking furious, because the only people who would get close enough to plant those devices would be someone we have given our trust to.

"Not yet, but we will. Hopefully before they have a chance to do it again," Blade grunts as he sits forward.

"Gino has taken over his duties." Since Gino left the hospital a week ago, he has been phoning me every day, telling me how good he feels. I told Blade that he could let him take over his duties when he thought he was ready. "Did he wear you out?" I ask, only to see Blade shake his head.

"You know, he can be a real nag," he complains as he stands to leave. "He was phoning me three times a day." I don't comment, as I know Blade doesn't really mind. I'm sure he was more than pleased to hand Gino his responsibilities back. "He has his men looking for the guy who shot him."

"If the guy is lucky, they will shoot him, because if Gino gets his hands on him, he will have a long, torturous death."

"Well, I'm out of here," Blade says as he walks towards the door.

"Ask Tommy to come here."

A few minutes later, I lift my hand, waving Tommy in. "You asked to see me, Boss?"

"You don't need to take Lola home tonight."

Tommy nods slowly, a concerned look in his eyes. "If you don't mind me asking, Boss, how is she getting home?"

"I'll take her." He nods. "Another thing, did you see what happened today?"

"I only saw when the car was racing away, but it was those Ukrainians. The guy with the gun had the tattoos that their soldiers have."

"Have you spoken to the police yet?" I ask as I sit back in my chair.

"Yes, but I didn't say anything about the Ukrainians."

"Good, you can go." Tommy leaves me to my thoughts, which aren't happy ones. There is a war going on. Someone in my club might be betraying us, and someone is scheming from the books. I lift the remote from my desk, pointing it at the flat screen on the wall. I scroll through the different cameras until I get to the one that captures the bar area. I see Lola behind the till. Two of the barmen are packing drinks. Everyone is preparing for the opening that will be in a couple minutes. I see Lola pull back her hair and tie it at the back of her head.

The beep of my phone has my eyes moving from her to my phone. "Yes?"

"We have a problem." Joey's voice has me sitting forward. "There has been another hit."

"Where?" I hope they didn't kill anyone.

"Our betting den downtown." I squeeze my eyes shut. That place is always full.

"Anyone killed?"

"Yeah, they shot up the place, Boss. Six dead and three are injured." Fuck, this is the consequence of a war, but that doesn't mean I have to like it.

"Who died, Joey?" I know my men all personally, and each one of them is important to the Capella family. I will make sure to go speak to the families myself. They will know that they will never have to worry about money. I will make sure to pay for everything, and I will let them know that we will make them pay.

"Santiago, Paulo, Tino. The other three were customers. Gloria, one of the waitresses, is injured. The other two injured are also customers." I feel the anger running through my body. I want to obliterate every single fucking Ukrainian.

"I'm coming." I stand and am about to leave when Joey stops me.

"This place is going to be crawling with cops. You don't want to be stuck in the middle of this." My whole body is tensing, but what Joey is saying is true.

"I want to be kept updated," I say, disconnecting the call. "Fuck." I rub at my face. I glance up at the screen that is still on and frown. Customers have already been let in, which has me apprehensive. With everything that has gone on today, maybe I should have closed Olympus. They have been staking out our businesses like we have theirs. They can decide to attack at any moment.

The number of people they would injure would be great, which would cripple Olympus for a long time. I am going to have to end this war. I don't want this dragging on, because we will be killing innocent people on both sides unnecessarily.

Lifting my phone, I dial. "Missing me already?" Blade quips.

"They hit the betting den." There is quiet on the other side for a few seconds.

"How many?" Blade asks.

"Six dead, three injured. I want a meeting with everyone at the restaurant tomorrow first thing. We're going to end this."

"I will get everyone there," Blade confirms before switching off. I lean my head back against the chair and close my eyes. It's going to be a long night. I look back at the screen and see Lola. I don't know what it is about her, but I can't seem to be able to keep my eyes off her. Grunting, I pull the files that Vito brought me earlier.

Going through each one, I get acquainted with Viktor's captains and their backgrounds. There is also a file on Viktor. Going through the file, I see that Viktor has been married twice, and both have died mysteriously. I am surprised he hasn't been arrested yet. It's clear he has his hand in a whole lot of murders.

He must have his finger on the police. That is the only way he hasn't been arrested yet. We have our share of dirty cops in our pocket, but we don't go around clearly murdering people, and I'm not a kingpin in the drug business like he is. It's clear that we shouldn't only be careful with Viktor's comeback but also about him setting us up for a fall. I will need to make sure we are smart, because from his file, it looks like he would easily set us up.

A couple hours later, I am still pouring over the files, when I hear the staff starting to leave. Looking at my watch, I realize that it's time to pack up, as Lola will be leaving soon. I have warned the boys to call her in here before she leaves. That's why when the door opens a few minutes later, I am not surprised to see one of the boys escorting Lola in. "She was going to leave, so I helped her here."

I tense. "How?" By my tone, he must realize he's skating on thin ice, because he shakes his head vehemently.

"He just stood in my way and didn't let me pass," Lola says as she takes a step in. "It's after my work hours. My contract doesn't state anything about overtime." I wave Carlos out as I lean back in my chair to look at Lola.

"You have a sassy mouth on you," I mutter as she approaches until she's standing before my desk. Her jeans moulding to her body, the tight black top she changed into doing nothing to detract from the perfect body underneath, and her breasts. My hardness professes to my liking of her plump breasts that fit my hand so perfectly. That nipple that pebbled at my touch. "I wanted to talk to you about what you said earlier, and then I'll take you home."

I see her body tensing, but she doesn't comment as she looks towards the chair and then takes a seat, waiting. "What did you mean about the skimming at the till?"

Her eyebrow lifts in suspicion, but after a minute, she shrugs and sits forward. "Are you testing me, or do you really not know?"

"If I knew, I wouldn't be asking you." I see her confusion, but then she shakes her head.

"Surely you must have noticed a discrepancy in the books." She frowns. "There is no way there wouldn't be. The number of orders that aren't added would have flagged up by now."

"Did you till all the orders today?"

"Of course. I told you I would," she says defensively.

"Did you log it in?" She nods. I turn to my laptop. Entering the accounting system, I go to today's figures and her specific till. Looking at the figure, I write it down on a pad I have on the desk. I then go to the same day last week that Julian was working and look at the figures there. There is a difference—a big difference. How was this not flagged earlier?

"It's quite a difference," Lola says as she looks at my scribbles on the notepad.

"Yes, it is," I mutter. "Now that I know about this, we will get to the bottom of it. Thank you for letting me know."

"To be honest, I thought you knew, and it was a way you were tweaking the accounts." I shake my head as I log out of my laptop. Pocketing my phone, I stand. I notice Lola immediately stands. I see her hand twisting the strap of her haversack nervously. It's good to know that I affect her as much as she affects me.

"Come here," I say when I'm standing next to the desk.

"Why?" she asks.

"You know why." I can sense her nervousness as she bites her bottom lip, a lip that I will kiss.

"This is a mistake," she mutters, but takes a step closer. I take hold of her upper arm before she can argue and pull her tight against my chest as my other hand entwines in her loose hair. Bending her head slightly back, I take her lips in a blistering kiss that leaves us both breathless. This woman is dangerous. She can make me forget everything in the split of a second.

Enough playing around. I let go of her hair, and my hands move to the hem of her body-fitting shirt. I pull it off. Her beautiful breasts encased in a beautiful lacy bra tease me as I throw the shirt on the floor. My fingers move to her bra, and I jerk enough to hear a rendering rip before her breasts jump out of the torn fabric. "What are you doing?" she mutters. Her hands start to rise to cover herself, but I grab her wrists, pulling them behind her back as I lower my head.

"Dom . . . we can't do this here." My name on her lips sounds right. The breathlessness there contradicts her words. I stroke my tongue over her pert nipple, hearing her sigh of pleasure. I feel her fingers in my hair, holding me close, my fingers move to the button on her jeans. Unbuttoning it, I pull down the zip.

Sliding my hand down the front of her jeans, I feel the smoothness of her skin. Damn, she's so fucking responsive that if I'm not careful, this first time won't last like I want it to last. My fingers feel the wetness between her legs, warning of her passion for me. I stroke her perky bud, feeling her body move under me, asking for more. My mouth on her breasts and my finger on her clit have her making the sexiest sounds that ignite my passion to new heights. I want to play with her body the whole night, but my self-control seems to be non-existent with her. Pulling my hand out from between her moistness, I hear her groan, which has me smiling. Taking hold of the waistband of her jeans, I pull them down. "Take them off," I mutter, as she needs to take off her shoes to get the jeans off.

She leans down, her ass up in the air for my view. Fuck, my woman is sexy. I unbutton my slacks, freeing myself into my hand. I am hard and dribbling with wanting her. She has the perfect ass to be spanked. Before she can turn around, I place my hands on her waist, sliding into her from the back.

"Dom," she murmurs as I bury myself deep within her body. Heaven, pure heaven. That's what this is. I start to move, slow at first, pulling out and then plunging in, hearing her moans as I move. The pressure building, I slide one hand over her hip down until I am touching her wetness again. Stroking my finger over her clit, I stroke it gently as I move within her, feeling her muscles start to contract around me. My other hand moves up her front until I'm holding her breast. Squeezing, I start to speed up my movements, feeling the end is near.

I can hear her gasps of pleasure, which has me pinching her nipple as I press down with my index finger on her little passion nub. "Dom, oh, oh," she gasps as her walls tighten around me, milking my seed until I'm the one grunting my release deep within her body. My movement slowing, my hands move once again towards her hips, holding her up as I feel her legs shaking in reaction to her release.

I have had sex with many women, maybe too many women, but never has it been like this. Lola doesn't know this yet, but she is mine.

LOLA 8

I should never have given in; I will just be a notch on his belt like so many others. I can feel my cheeks burning as I slide my shirt on without my bra, as it is completely torn and useless. "I will get you another one." I look up at him to see his stubble from not shaving in a day. I can still feel the heat on my breasts and neck from his kisses and how it scraped so deliciously across my skin. Dom is a handsome man; his chocolate-brown eyes are still heaving with the passion we just shared.

"No, I don't want you to buy me anything." I see him frown at my reply as I lift my hands to try to bring some kind of control to my bed hair.

"I broke it, I will pay for it."

"I swear if you give me money, I will hit you."

He raises a brow, and then his lips kick up in amusement. He places his index finger under my chin, his thumb stroking my cheek. "So proud," he murmurs. "I won't pay you for what we just did. We both wanted it. We both want it; this isn't finished, my *bella* Lola."

I shake my head; we can't do this again. "This was wrong. We can't do this again." I see him tense, a frown appearing, and then his lips are lowering again, and he is taking my lips in a breathless kiss that leaves me disorientated. How does he do this? How can I forget everything and everyone when he touches me?

"You are wrong. This will happen again, and many times. I want you, Lola. You have intrigued me from the moment I saw you. You are mine."

"I'm not your property. I am just working for you to pay off my papa's debt," I say angrily, pulling away from him, but his hands shoot out and grab my waist, bringing me close to him again.

"You are mine now, don't doubt it." He takes my lips again in a possessive kiss that at first, I try to fight, but in the end, it overpowers my senses. When he finally lifts his head, I am breathing heavily, and my body is craving his, wanting everything and more of what we did earlier.

"Let's go before I take you again. We would never leave here today." He lets go of my body. Taking a step back, he looks around as if to make sure he has everything with him before placing his hand on my back and guiding me towards the door. When he opens the door, I realize that the two guards must have heard us inside. Oh, how embarrassing. I lower my head as we make it outside, the two men following us.

Dom opens the passenger door to his very expensive and sporty-looking car. Climbing in, I read the name Shelby on the steering wheel. Men and their toys. It doesn't matter if they're poor or wealthy, all of them like their fast cars.

"Everyone is going to think I'm easy," I mutter angrily. I see his surprised look as he looks over at me as he starts the car.

"No one will think that. Why would they?"

I look at his surprised expression in scorn. "Really? You think after your men heard us in the office, people aren't going to start talking?" I cross my arms over my chest as I turn my head to look out the window, seeing the two men pulling up before us in a car of their own, not as fancy as this one, but fast just the same, and then I see another car with what looks like Dom's men, too, sitting in another car, waiting for us to pull out of the guarded parking lot.

"My office is soundproof. No one heard nothing, and everyone will soon know you are mine. They will know not to speculate."

"I have told you; I am not yours. I do not belong to anyone except myself." Dom grunts in annoyance. He doesn't say anything else until I interrupt the silence, as I notice we're not taking the way home.

"This isn't the way to my house," I mutter, looking at the upscale neighbourhood we are entering. He doesn't answer as he continues driving. "Dom, where are you taking me? It's late and I'm tired."

"You're going to be staying with me." At his words, I tense. What the hell does he think he's doing?

"No, I'm not. Turn around and take me back." When he doesn't immediately comply, my anger rises. "My dad is going to be worried. I'm not going to stay with you. Now turn around." He turns into a long driveway. When the house comes into view, I stare. He lives here? It's beautiful. I don't know why, but I imagined him staying in an upscale apartment with all the commodities nearby, and with all the property that surrounds the house, it's secluded from any prying eyes. He comes to a stop in front of the double doors.

"I'm not staying here," I mutter as he gets out of the car, but he doesn't even hesitate. Walking around the car, he opens the passenger door. Placing a hand on my upper arm, he drags me out of the car until I am standing next to him. "I'm not staying here, Dom," I say again. "My father needs me at home."

"You either walk on your own two feet or I carry you inside, and that my men will see." At his threat, I tense. Looking over my shoulder, I see the men standing next to their cars, looking around the property to identify any hidden threats.

Muttering to myself, I start making my way up towards the house. I sense Dom walking right behind me. I am about to open the door, when suddenly, I am being thrust behind Dom. His body is tense, and I know immediately that there is some kind of danger that he is sensing that I am not. "What's wrong?"

"Shh," he mutters as he opens the door. He has pulled a gun from the back of his waistband and is now holding it before him as he steps inside. The first thing I see is the beautiful foyer with its shiny marble floors and the sweeping stairs, and then I freeze as from the corner of my eye, I see a man lying in a pool of blood. I look behind me, only to find the four men surrounding us, their guns also drawn. What the hell have I gotten myself into?

Dom walks inside. I reluctantly follow, keeping as close to him as possible. He looks over his shoulder at the men, indicating for two to go one way and the others the other way. Great, now we're alone here in the middle. I look up the stairs, expecting anyone to jump up at any moment and start shooting. "Stay close," Dom mutters.

He walks towards the clearly dead man lying on the ground. Squatting, he places his fingers at his throat to feel his pulse. I don't know who this man was, but it's clear that Dom was close to him by the anger and pain I can see on his face. Two of the men come back and then climb the stairs, I'm guessing to make sure that the house is safe. Dom stands, turns, and looks around us. He tenses and lifts his gun when we hear running footsteps from outside.

Two men rush inside, their guns drawn, only to come to a stop when they see us.

"Boss," one of them mutters, and then looks down to see the dead man on the floor.

"What happened here?" Dom asks. His voice is a soft growl filled with rage.

"We heard a shot. When we got here, Alberto was dead. We have combed the whole area. There is no one."

"House is clear," the men who went upstairs say as they come to a stop at the bottom.

"I want everyone here now," Dom says in a tone that brooks no argument.

"Will do, Boss."

"What's happening here?" I ask Dom as he takes my upper arm and starts to guide me upstairs. I can feel his tense muscles as my arm rubs against him as he climbs up the stairs.

"We are at war. Today, they decided to attack us, but just because they won a fight doesn't mean they have won the war."

"You have placed me in the middle of a war?" I mutter, only to have him stop and turn me towards him. By the tick in his jaw, I can tell that I should have kept my mouth shut, as I don't think he's in the mood for questioning.

"I will make sure you are safe. Nothing will happen to you." He pulls me to him and kisses me. It's a short, possessive kiss. I can see the pain in his eyes. I don't know who that man was to him, but it's clear that his death has touched him. I want to hug him close and try to appease some of the pain, but before I can move, he is again walking down a corridor until he is opening double doors into a room that is surely the size of my papa's sitting room and kitchen put together.

I can't stay here. I need to make sure that Papa is fine, but I won't fight him any more today, as it is clear that he has more than enough going on. I will send a message to Papa so when he wakes up, he knows that I am fine. I look around to see a huge bed, with double doors leading to what looks like a balcony. There are two beautiful hand-carved side tables below a chandelier reflecting like diamonds everywhere it shines.

"Your room is beautiful," I state. He looks over his shoulder as he discards his jacket and makes his way into what looks like it could be a bathroom.

"It's your room, too, now," he says, disappearing inside. I ignore his comment. Instead, I follow him to find him unbuttoning his shirt.

"Who was that man?"

He takes a deep breath before he answers. "When I was young, he was my bodyguard, and then with time, he became one of my advisors." I see his magnificent naked body for the first time, every muscle clearly defined as he moves. Oh man, he's one sexy specimen. "Join me," he states as he steps into a huge shower, the water running down his body.

"Dom, we need to talk about this," I mutter as I point around.

"Give it a break, Lola. Just get in here."

I'm not someone who is ordered around, and he seems to like doing that.

"I'll wait outside." He grunts in annoyance but doesn't say anything. As I step into the bedroom, the door bursts open. I jump in surprise. "Are you guys trying to give me a heart attack today?" I ask angrily as I face Blade, but he seems as surprised as me.

"What are you doing here?" he asks, but then he must have heard the water running, because he grunts.

"I would also like to know," I mutter, which earns me a raised brow from Blade. I see his eyes run down my body, not missing a thing.

"Wait downstairs." At Dom's statement, I snap around to see him walking out with a towel draped around his waist. Blade frowns, but he doesn't say anything as he turns and leaves.

"Do you know who killed him?"

Dom shrugs. "I don't know who the man was, but I know who sent him. This will end today."

I feel a chill running up my spine. Walking towards him, I place my hand on his chest, feeling his body tense at the touch. "I'm sorry." I watch the pain he is trying to hide flood his features. I'm a sucker for anyone in distress. Placing my arms around his waist, I lay my head on his bare chest, holding him close. I can hear his heartbeat below my ear. For some reason, the rhythm calms my worries. His arms are around my body, and he holds me tight. Seeing this sensitive side to a man like Dom has my outlook of him changing. I know he's a hardened man, a man who will do anything for the Capella family, but seeing him like this gives me hope that he still has a soft side to him, a side that bleeds when wounded.

"Rest. No one will bother you here. I have things to take care of, but I will be back later." He pulls away. Looking down at me, he tweaks my nose before he turns and opens a door that leads to a walk-in closet. He pulls out a black suite with a light-grey shirt.

"What if the police want to ask me questions?"

He raises a brow and then shakes his head. "Lola, rest. There will be no one interrupting your sleep."

Well, of course not. Why would he call the police when he's thinking of doing the same to whoever came into his house and killed his friend? How did I get involved in all this?

I look around at the men in the office. We have just gone through the plans for the attack. In all the years we have been together, never have I felt the burden on my shoulders like I do today. Men's lives are at stake, possible lives of innocent people. I will fight until my last breath for the men who now sit before me. They have given me their lives, their unconditional trust. I will not let them down. I am the head of the Capella family, and as such, I will make sure that we rise above this threat and come out victorious on the other side.

I have given them their orders; we are all attacking at the same time. We will make sure to cripple their business, cripple their very existence. Viktor is mine. I will deal with him myself. He wants to take what isn't his, wants to wound me by taking those close to me. I will make him pay. I will make him feel the wrath of the Capella family in its entirety. He will know that he chose the wrong beast to poke.

"I want it all done at the same time," I state, looking around. "Your men are to be ready in two hours, and I expect to see all of you back here when it's done."

"Let's go show them who they messed with," Vito says as he leans forward.

I point a finger at him. "Don't be a cowboy, Vito. Do what you need to and get out of there. Remember, these fuckers might have cameras. Make sure no one gets caught on them."

"We have everything ready; we will make them pay for what they did to Alberto and the others today," Joey says.

"I think you should stay here. Not a good idea to have you facing Viktor." I understand Blade is just thinking about my wellbeing and the family, but this is my war, and I won't send my men to fight a war I am not prepared to fight in.

"I'm going," I state, looking at Blade. I know the others won't argue with me, but Blade will try his luck. He won't do it in front of the others. He will wait before he tries again, but on this, I won't change my mind. It is my right to kill Viktor. "We are done here. Go get ready."

"Gino," I call as he's about to walk out the door. "Try not to get shot again."

He looks over his shoulder and grins as he shrugs. "Where's the fun in that?" he says before he continues on his way.

"I'm not changing my mind, Blade," I mutter as Blade continues sitting.

"I didn't think you would. What I want to know is are you leaving Lola here while you are away?" I look at him. What does he mean? "Can you trust her?"

"Yes." He shrugs as he stands. "Blade, she's mine."

He stops and then sits back down. "What do you mean?"

"She's mine. She will be living here going forward." I see his look of surprise, which I understand, as I have never been with a woman for long, and especially never had any of them move into my house.

"I knew you were hot for her when I saw your eyes on her all the time." He stands again, and this time, he makes his way towards the door. There, he turns. "See you later, brother," he says before he leaves. Closing my eyes, I lean my head back against the chair. This will be the end of this war. I hear a slight step. Snapping my eyes open, I see Lola standing in the doorway, the light shining behind her.

"Why aren't you sleeping?" I ask, noticing that she's still wearing the clothes from earlier.

"Do you really think I can sleep with everything that has happened today?" she asks as she approaches. Her eyes run over my features.

"Come here," I say, and to my surprise, she does, coming to stand next to my chair. I take hold of her arm, pulling. She yelps as she falls into my lap.

"You're such a barbarian," she mutters as she leans her head against my chest. The action has my heart racing. The only use I've ever had for women is the sexual type. This is a completely different experience for me, like her hugging me upstairs. I don't know what Lola is doing to me, but I like that she feels the need to come to me for comfort.

Raising my hand, I stroke her head. The feeling of having her close calms the anger that has been racing through my body since the moment I walked into the house and saw

Alberto lying on the floor in a pool of his own blood. She was right when we walked upstairs. I have placed her in danger. I should never have brought her into my life, especially at a time like this, but now that she is in it, I can't let her go, not that I would have. She will be safe here; I will make sure of it.

I don't know how long we are sitting here like this before Tommy appears at the door and points to his watch. Lifting my arm, I look at my wristwatch to see that it's time to be leaving. Nodding, I stand, pulling Lola tight against my chest. I hear her murmur, but she doesn't awaken. I like that she feels safe in my arms. She fell asleep nearly instantaneously when she came into my arms earlier, which tells me that she was scared but was too stubborn to admit it.

I will make sure to make it safe again for her. I don't want my woman scared of what we might find when coming home. Walking up the stairs and to my room, I lay her down gently on the bed as not to wake her. Hopefully when she awakens, I will be back, victorious, and this war will be over. I turn and make my way back downstairs. Tommy is standing by the door when I approach. He hands me my gun that I slot into the waistband of my slacks. He then holds out my other gun that slots into the holster on my side, and finally, the one that I slip into the holster under my slacks leg.

"We're ready, Boss," Tommy says as I step outside to see fifteen of my men standing next to the four cars we will be travelling in. Some of them already have their balaclavas rolled up on their heads. I take mine from Paulo as I walk past. Before getting into the car, I stop.

"I want you all to be careful today. Make sure that no one will be able to identify you after, and stay alive. We will make them pay for the deaths they caused today; we will show them that they messed with the wrong *familia*." With those words, I step into the car, hearing the men call out the Capella family name as they place their right hands over their hearts.

"Are the other men in place here at the house?" I ask Tommy as we start making our way down the driveway. I ordered that enough men stay at the house to guard Lola. I want to make sure that whatever happened earlier doesn't happen again.

"Yes, Boss." We drive through the quiet streets, making our way towards Viktor's apartment building. When we park outside, I pull the balaclava down over my face as I slip out of the car, making my way up the stairs to the entrance. Each of my men have been briefed on what they need to do. I trust their judgement and know that I won't need to worry about anything from their side being missed. I walk into the foyer, five men following me. My guns are all still in place. One of my men opens fire and shoots the two men standing at reception. Another of my men shoots the man by the lifts. Making sure not to alert anyone until necessary, we all have silencers on our weapons, so the noise is minimal.

I slip into the lift, and three of my men follow me. Two will be standing guard downstairs in the foyer in case anyone we are not expecting makes an appearance. When the lift finally opens its door on the top floor, I slip my gun out of the back of my waistband. It is time to end this war and to make Viktor pay for having thought that he could attack the Capella family.

As the lift doors open, I see two of Viktor's men sitting on a leather couch. One of them looks over his shoulder as the doors open. Before he can pull out his gun, my men shoot both dead. I continue walking past the sitting room and down the corridor. I can hear voices from just ahead. As we approach, one of Viktor's men walks into the corridor. When he sees us, he shouts, pulling out his gun, but before he succeeds, he is dead.

There is scattering as whoever was inside the room the man just walked out of prepares to protect himself. Two of my men rush in. There is a shot and then pops from my men. I continue making my way down to the end of the corridor where I know Viktor is. By now, he knows I am coming, with the noise from the shot, but this will be over soon. Standing to the side, I open the door; I hear a *whoosh* and am just in time to see Viktor closing a door to the side of his room.

Walking towards the door, I frown as I realize he has a panic room. Why the fuck wasn't this in the file? This isn't how I wanted it, but it will have to do. "Light it up," I mutter. I hear movement and am guessing that one of my men went into the kitchen to find something to set this place on fire. Viktor will die today, and all his men, too. This war will be at an end. I hear the crackling sound and know that a fire has started. Looking over my shoulder, I see the bed is going up in flames, and so are the curtains. "Over here," I say, making sure we don't miss him.

I turn as my men make sure that the fire catches. Making my way down the corridor again, I see the expensive paintings on the walls, the sculptures he has around the house. No one would ever have thought by looking at the apartment that everything in here was bought with drug money. Making my way towards the main door, I wait, listening to the fire crackling. My men make their way towards me. When the last one is near me, he throws a light on the curtains near us. When the fire starts to crackle up the curtains, we turn and make our way to the lift.

Viktor won't make it out of this. We are done here and hopefully at peace again for a long time. When I am back in the car, I pull the balaclava off my head and slip my phone out of my pocket to see a message from Vito. *See you tomorrow.* I smile as I think of his pleased expression. This is what Vito lives for. Give him a fight and he is happy.

Arriving at home, I make my way inside. Looking towards where Alberto was lying earlier, I see that everything has been cleaned and now looks like nothing happened there. A great man was killed all because of greed. There is a lot to be done tomorrow. There is a thief in the club who needs to be caught, and when that person is caught, we will know who was placing the listening devices in my office and why.

I have arranged for Alfredo's sponsor to go stay with him to make sure he stays on the straight and narrow until they are both happy that he won't relapse. I will need to tell Lola what I have done, but I think once she realises that it's what is best for her father, she won't argue much. I'm not doing this out of the goodness of my heart. I am doing this because I know that Lola would never leave her father alone to come stay here, but like this, she will have no option.

I shake my head when I think how spirited Lola is. I know she will fight me in what she thinks is right, and I don't expect anything less. That is why she fascinates me. Lola has filled my every waking hour with thoughts of her since the minute I met her. I will make sure that she realizes that no matter how much she fights me, we are meant to be together. She was born to be by my side. I know that she will keep me from deviating from what is right. She is the woman I want by my side, a woman I know I can trust because I know that as soon as Lola takes someone into her circle of family, she gives them her complete trust and honesty.

I will do right by her, but first, I think she will make me fight every inch of the way before she finally accepts that she is mine.

Today, there is once again peace, but for how long?

THE END.

REIGN

Capella Family (Book 2)

Reign

A strong woman scorned is a force to be reckoned with!

GINO

The past has driven my anger, and molded my life, making me the man that I am today. Hard, deadly, and only loyal to the Capella Famiglia. When everything died around me only the Famiglia stood by me, only the Famiglia were there. I lost all hope of ever finding someone to love, my life is not for the faint hearted, I never thought there was a woman that could live this life with me, but now I have hope, maybe, there is a woman strong enough to withstand the horrors of my life.

AMORE

Being a woman surrounded by hard, violent men, one learns how to be strong, how to stand up for myself and fight for what I believe. Loyalty, family and love is what drives me, it's what makes me strong, doing what is necessary to save those around me is what pushes me to do what I did, it can either go very right or very wrong!

AMORE 1

"Are you sure about this, mia figlia?"

I look over my shoulder towards where Papa is standing in the doorway staring at me. I smile. "Of course." Turning towards him, I shrug. "This was my idea, everything will be fine, you will see." I see his shoulders relax slightly. I know that he won't show his worry to anyone else, but as his daughter, he has always been more open with me. Being the Padrino of one of the most influential crime families in Italy, he cannot afford to show vulnerability because the other crime families will eat him alive.

"If Gino does not treat you right, you tell me, you hear me, Amore?" I make my way towards him.

The lines next to his eyes are evidence that he's worried about my future.

"You know I can take care of myself," I say as I slide my arms around his waist and lay my head against his chest like I used to do when I was a little girl. His arms hug me close. I might be all grown up, and now twenty-five, but he will always consider me his little girl.

"Yes, I know you can, but you are going to be living with a different famiglia. They will be suspicious initially, so if you have any problems, come home."

The reason why I decided to join our two famiglia's was to strengthen our position within the underworld. The Nessun Perdono Crime Famiglia is strong in its own right, but it's nothing like the Capella Famiglia.

I met Gino at a charity ball. There was chemistry between us from the minute our eyes clashed, but because of our families, we have kept away.

When I heard Leo, my older brother and the next in line to be Boss of The Nessun Perdono crime Famiglia, telling everyone at the meeting what predicament we were in, I found the perfect opportunity to get to know Gino, and to suggest to everyone that we could join the two Famiglias in matrimony.

Since the death of Constantine, one of the other famiglia's Bosses, his son Matteo, has decided to wage war against us. He wants to be the strongest Famiglia around, but first, he needs to conquer us before he can go after the Capella Famiglia. He knows that it will be suicide to try to stand against Dominique.

Papa refused to even consider it at first, but being the stubborn, hard-headed woman that I am, I decided to meet with Dominique, the Capella Famiglia Boss, and propose a deal to him that would have been hard to refuse.

One thing I wasn't expecting was him not agreeing immediately. As the Boss of the famiglia, I would have thought he would have agreed to the union himself, but out of respect for his Capo and friend, he asked Gino first if he would agree to the union.

My respect for Dominique grew, knowing that he isn't intimidated by his Capo's or Underboss' power within his famiglia,

I was surprised when I received a call from Gino himself, agreeing to the plan. He asked that I give him a time and place and promised me he would be there. His deep voice had me thinking of dark nights and his strong arms around me.

This was a month ago, and usually the daughter of the Boss of one of the main crime famiglia's in Italy being married, would be a huge affair that would last for days, but because of the unrest among the Famiglia's at the moment, we are going to have a quiet ceremony with only the Capo's from both Famiglia's, the Underbosses, Dom, and Papa present.

I was surprised to have received a contract from Dominique. Not so much the contract because I was expecting that, but the content of the contract. It stated that we are to make it a real marriage in all sense of the word.

When I first proposed this idea to Papa, I thought that this marriage was going to be in name only, for appearances and for the good of the Famiglia's, but after the contract, I get the impression that Gino would like to try to make this work which I am not averse to.

Ever since the day that I saw him at the ball, my thoughts have been plagued with images of him. He is one handsome devil, but there is a dangerous aura about him that most of the mafia men have. With Gino, it seems somehow deeper. There is a stillness about him that intrigues me.

"I will be fine, Papa. Now let's go before the groom thinks that I got cold feet," I tease as I lean forward to kiss his cheek. My Papa is a hard, unforgiving man that lives by his beliefs. He has instilled those principles in both his children. I might be a woman, but I live and breathe the Famiglia values.

"Anyone that knows you, will know that you are not one to get cold feet. Once you decide on something, come hell or high water, you, my dear figlia, will get it."

GINO 2

"I heard she's a real man-eater."

Glancing at Vito, I raise my brow. I know what people say about my bride to be, but I have never been one to run away from a challenge. Besides, I like feisty females.

When I first saw Amore, everything around me stilled. I felt a peace internally that I haven't felt in a very long time—if ever. My woman has a regal air about her that obscures the presence of any women around her.

Her beautiful, long, silky brown hair made my fingers twitch to stroke it. Her dark blue eyes are intense with intelligence and internal strength.

"That's the point; I think Gino here wants to be nibbled on," Blade teases as he walks into the room past me, slapping me on the back.

Vito grins at Blade's comment as he leans towards me to pull at the knot on my tie. "Today this needs to look perfect," he mutters as he starts to re-knot my tie. Vito, Blade, Dominique, and Joey have been in my life from a very young age, when I was struggling the most with the loss of my family.

Seeing my family being gunned down when I was fourteen changed my life, it changed the person that I became. There is fury that runs through my veins, and I don't know if I will be any good to Amore as a husband. I'm not a good man. I'm hard and unforgiving of those that attack me and those I hold dear.

I need a strong woman beside me. A woman that will understand my drive for justice. A woman that has the same values as me, and from what I have heard about Amore, she is the perfect woman for someone like me.

I never thought that I would be getting married, or find a woman that would fit in with the type of life I live. My way of life is dangerous—traitorous in so many respects.

When Dom approached me with Amore's proposal, I was taken aback. I am the last man I would have thought that she would have gone for; not only because I had never spoken to her before the day I phoned her to accept her proposal, but because I am known for being intense and dangerous to all.

Amore is a beautiful woman, I know she could have her pick from many men, but she decided to choose me. I made sure that she understood that I would accept her proposal only if it were a marriage in all sense of the word.

Today she becomes my wife, and even if we drive each other crazy, this has been our decision, and we will live by it. There will be no cheating, no side-line arrangements for us. If we want to be happy in our marriage, we are going to have to make it work.

I know that there is an attraction between us—an attraction that I'm sure with time, we can make it into something more. I have only seen my bride once, but that moment has plagued me with visions of her beautiful dark blue eyes looking at me with longing ever since.

"Are you ready?" I turn my head to see Dom and Joey walking in.

"Si."

Dom approaches until he is standing a foot away from me. "Are you sure you want to do this?"

"You have asked me this before. Yes, I am sure."

Dom nods, raising his hand before he places it on my shoulder. "I would never have thought you'd be the first to get married," Dom says as he inclines his head towards Vito. "I thought he would."

"Me! Why me?" Vito asks with a raised brow.

"Because you're a sucker for punishment." At Dom's comment, I smile when I see Vito's disgruntled look. It's true that Vito is a lady's man, but I know that Dom is pulling his leg, because out of all of us, I think he's the one that will never get married because he has way too much fun being a single man to ever think of tying himself down.

"The Nessun Perdono are here, we should go out." I look over towards where Blade is leaning against the wall looking out the window.

"Okay, let's do this," I say as I look at Dom again to receive his nod of approval. Even though we all grew up together, we still have the respect expected with one in a position like Dom has. To be the Boss of a crime famiglia, like the Capella Famiglia, isn't easy.

Dom needs to know that he has the respect and loyalty of those around him. Becoming the Boss at his age was unexpected, but he has held the famiglia together with sound decisions, and I will stand by him no matter what.

Walking out towards where the priest is standing at the front of the chapel, I see Leo, the Nessun Perdone Underboss, and two of their Capo's standing to one side. When they see us, they nod in greeting and then take a seat.

Standing at the front of the chapel, I turn to see Dom has taken a seat in the front row. Blade is sitting to his right and Joey to his left with Vito sitting right behind him.

This is the only family I have left. My aunt that took me in after my parents and sister were gunned down, died three years ago. She was the only one left, she became a mother to me after everything that happened. She didn't like my connection with the famiglia, but she accepted it. I wish she was here today to see the woman I'm marrying— a woman that belongs to this life. A woman that will stand up to my bullshit and put me in my place.

My aunt always said that I needed a strong woman to set me straight. Well, she might be getting her wish. The chapel doors open, and the wedding march starts to play. I can feel a knot in my stomach, even though I have accepted this arrangement, it is a new chapter of my life. It's a new responsibility—a wish that I thought wasn't achievable.

I always wanted a family—my own family, but the memories of what happened to me has always stopped me from pursuing that wish. Now, with this opportunity arising, it seems like I have no reason not to try to make it work.

From what I have gathered, Amore is a strong, independent woman that is used to this life. She is used to manipulation and conniving happening around her. I just hope that she isn't like that, I hope that she is just and true to our values.

I see Santiago, the head of the Nessun Perdone crime famiglia, come into view. His steel grey hair is shining from the sun outside. This is going to be my father-in-law, and part of my family after today. He is a hard son of a bitch. He rules over his famiglia with an iron fist, but he loves his children, and for him to agree to this union, means that he is feeling cornered by the threat that Matteo is posing.

We're not worried about Matteo, he is a small fish in a big pond. At the moment, we have more pressing matters to worry about, such as the war with the Ukrainian Mafia.

But even though we are under no real threat from Matteo, we have decided that it is better to have Santiago as our ally then as a threat.

Our families together will be undefeated, and Matteo will realize that. In the meantime, we will request that Santiago help us with the issue we are having with the Ukrainian's.

My thoughts come to an abrupt stop when I see Amore step up next to her father. Her sexy body is encased in a beautiful flowing white dress that does nothing to hide the curves under it. Her silky brown hair is tied up on the top of her head in a messy bun, tendrils of wispy strands are falling around her face. The distance doesn't allow for me to see the expression in her eyes, but soon she is walking towards me, her steps sure, her eyes on me as she approaches.

When they are just a couple of steps away, I step forward to take her from her father. The moment our hands touch, a flash of energy races up my arm and across my body. I feel a quiver in her fingers, which tells me that she felt it, too. Our eyes clash and hold, hers is a stormy blue, hiding deep emotions and passion.

"Amore," I say, trying her name out loud for the first time.

"Gino." Her husky voice is low and intense. Turning, I guide Amore before the priest.

"We are gathered here…" the priest begins. They are words that will bind our two strong families—words that will bind our two lives for eternity.

AMORE 3

Today has been intense. Gino and I hardly had any time to talk to each other. From the moment the priest announced us as man and wife, Papa and Dom have been talking about the way forward, and what they expect from each other.

As all the Capo's and the two underbosses are here, they decided to hold the meeting while we are having our wedding meal. As the daughter of Santiago, I am used to these meetings. I'm aware of everything that is happening in Papa's organization, but I was hoping that at least for today, we could have had this meal in peace without any business talk, but I should have known better.

Gino has been quietly listening to the conversation and comments from the others, only commenting when asked. Sitting here beside him gives me a chance to analyse him without making it obvious, but I have a feeling that Gino is always aware of everything around him.

His dark brown, nearly black hair has been cut since the last time I saw him, his green eyes taking everything in as he listens, he seems to be sitting relaxed in his chair, but I think that his stillness hides the deadliness in him.

"... burn their fucking balls." Those last words catch my attention, which has me turning my attention to one of my father's Capo's that voiced them.

"You know, this is supposed to be a celebration and not a horror show. I think we have spoken about business for long enough, don't you all think?" I've had enough of listening to their plots against their enemies.

"You are right, Figlia. How remiss of us." Papa stands, glass in hand as he stretches out his hand in a toast. "May your union strengthen our bond and bring us all peace." Everyone lifts their glass and then takes a drink. I'm surprised when I suddenly feel Gino's hand over mine and he's standing with his glass in hand as Papa sits down.

"A toast to my wife that has brought us all together. A woman that has confronted all the men at this table, and that holds the courage of a lioness. May I be worthy of her courage and vision." His toast has my heart racing at the fact that he appreciates the reason behind why I proposed this union, but mostly, it's racing at the fact that he called me his wife for the very first time.

After drinking from my glass, I stiffen when I see him turn, and instead of sitting, he bends down and touches his lips to mine. It's a fleeting kiss, but the touch of his warm lips against mine has me catching my breath.

"I think it's time we left. What do you say?" he asks just a breath away from me.

"Yes." I have never been one to be tongue tied, but Gino has my stomach fluttering with nerves just like a teenager. He straightens, pulling me up as he does, then turns to face the others that are looking at us with different expressions on their faces.

"If you will all excuse us, it's time that my wife and I get to know each other." There's no reason to act as if we are madly in love with each other because everyone around this table knows exactly why we got married today.

We say our goodbyes and soon Gino is guiding me towards his black Ford Mustang. I see two of the Capella soldiers standing guard near the car. When they see us, they nod to Gino and then make their way towards a car parked behind his.

Gino guides me into the car. When we are finally on our way, I look over at Gino, seeing the frown on his face as he drives.

"Why me?"

His question catches me by surprise

"Why not you?"

"You could have chosen Vito or Joey. They are more suited to be a husband, but you chose me." He glances at me before looking back at the road.

"Vito is too flamboyant for me, and Joey doesn't do anything for me." I have promised myself to always be as truthful as possible with Gino. I don't want to start a marriage with lies.

"You don't even know me."

I shrug as I smile. "I might not know you, but you seem more intense, less approachable."

"And that makes me marriage material?" he sounds suspicious.

"Let's just say that you fit in better."

His lips raise in a smile. "You have no idea who I am." I hear the conviction in his voice, it tells me that what he's saying he believes whole heartedly. "I'm a hard man, Amore, I don't take fools lightly."

"That's good because I don't think I could be married to a spineless man with no convictions."

"Amore, you are now part of the Capella Famiglia, I need to know that I can trust you." He pulls into the driveway of a grand house, then he turns to look at me once we are parked in front.

"Can I trust you?"

He raises a brow at my question, but nods.

"I will not betray you. I take my vows deeply. Can I expect the same from you?" One thing that he can always expect from me is directness. I don't believe in dancing around an issue, but discussing it and coming to a consensus.

Gino raises his hand to my cheek, his thumb stroking it gently as he looks into my eyes. "You are beautiful."

My heart is racing as his head nears, his eyes never leaving mine as he watches my expressions. When our lips touch, it's like an explosion of senses. His hand slides to the back of my head, pulling me closer. The kiss deepens as he takes possession of my every breath. I raise my hand to his neck, feeling the heat under my palm.

Both of our breaths are staggered, and when we finally break apart, his eyes are filled with passion when he looks at me. "Looks like we will get along just fine."

I frown. "I hope you aren't thinking that all I'm good for is sex, because I can tell you right now, that won't happen. I have always..." before I can finish my tirade, he is kissing me again, making my thoughts fly out of my mind.

I have been kissed many times before, but never have I been so completely overwhelmed by a kiss like I am now. It is evident that Gino knows exactly what he is doing. It looks like the art of seduction is something he has in abundance.

"Let's go inside," he says when he finally breaks the kiss. Turning, he exits the car and walks around to open my door, helping me out. His hand slides down my back to the base of my spine, guiding me up the three steps before the double doors. The doors open and there stands a middle-aged woman with a beaming smile on her face.

"You are home," she says excitedly.

"Teresa, I thought you would have been in bed by now." She shakes her head, dismissing Gino's words. It's amusing how he lets her shush him.

"You must be Amore; I've been so excited to meet you." Teresa has such an open, cheerful disposition that I immediately feel comfortable around her.

"Hello, Teresa, nice to meet you." Mama died when I was eight. There has been no other woman in my life because Papa never remarried. We have an Aunt Tamara, but she isn't much of a mother figure. Having someone like Teresa in my life might turn out to be interesting.

"Come, come, Gino, bring your wife inside; stop standing in the doorway." I see Gino shake his head from out of the corner of my eyes.

"Maybe if we weren't accosted as soon as we got home, we would already be inside." Gino's comment has Teresa shaking her head as she takes my hand, pulling me inside.

"Men," she mutters good naturedly.

"Teresa was my aunt's friend. she took care of her when she became ill. She lives in the cottage at the back of the property with her husband Thomas," Gino explains.

Teresa lets go of my hand when we reach a spacious, well-furnished sitting room. "Your aunt would have been so happy that you have finally settled down," Teresa says with a sad smile. "All she wanted was for you to find someone you could love." She then looks at me. "You treat him good. He is a hard man, but he has a good heart, our Gino has." She pats my arm before turning away from us. "Now I'm going home before Thomas comes looking for me." She starts to take her leave. "I will be in early to make breakfast," she calls just before exiting the room.

Turning my head, I look over at Gino who's still slightly bemused at Teresa. She seems like a great person and I'm sure I will love her. I see Gino shaking his head in amusement.

"I like her," I say, surprised because I usually take a while to warm up to people.

"Yes, Teresa is special," Gino says with a shrug as he walks towards a cabinet full of drinks. "Would you like a drink?" At any other time, I would have had one, but I hardly ate at dinner and I want to make sure that I have my wits around me, when spending my first night with Gino.

"No thank you."

He nods as he pours himself a whiskey. Turning towards me again, I see his eyes move over my body in a slow fervent perusal, igniting a deep passion that courses through my body.

"What Teresa said is true, I am a hard man." He takes a step closer, his eyes intense as they clash with mine.

"She also said that you have a good heart."

He raises a brow. "Don't believe everything you hear."

That has me smiling. "Don't worry, I plan to find out for myself exactly how you are."

He places his glass on the coffee table, and then he's approaching me again with a determined look on his face.

"Well, Wife, no time like the present," he growls before his hand is slipping around the back of my neck, pulling me flush against him. His head lowers and then everything around me vanishes as his lips connect with mine.

The kiss is as intense as the man himself. His other arm comes around my waist, holding me tight. I can feel the evidence of his arousal pressing against me as his kiss guides my passion to bubbling heights.

GINO 4

Stepping back, I break the kiss only to hear Amore groan in frustration. This woman is going to either be my salvation or the death of me. Leaning down, I pick her up against me. "Time to go upstairs."

"I can walk," she murmurs.

"But it's faster my way." My words have her grinning as I take the steps two at a time.

"Nice to know that I have such a strong husband."

Her humour has me slowing, only now realizing that I'm acting like a teenage boy with his first girlfriend. Since the moment I saw Amore at the Ball, she has been on my mind—everything about her turns me on.

Entering the room, I let her legs slide down onto the ground, her arms glide around my neck as she lifts her face for my kiss. Her sweet fragrance surrounds me. My hands move to her back to pull down the zip of her sexy, body-fitted wedding dress. I slide my hand in where the unfastened dress has fallen open, stroking my fingers down her back.

Our kiss deepens, heightening both our passion even more. My body vibrates with anticipation as she rubs against me every time we move. Lifting my head, I push against her, which forces her to take a step back, then another, and another until the back of her legs hit the edge of the mattress. Placing my hand on the front of her dress, I pull her towards me. At the same time, I push her gently with the other hand, making her lose her balance. She gasps, falling back. The dress slips off her arms as I pull it down to her waist and then off completely.

It's my turn to take in a deep breath when I see her beautiful body encased in the sexy pearl-colored lingerie, breasts teasing me behind the sheer silky fabric that does nothing to conceal her rosy nipples. Garters attached to stockings made of the same fabric hug her juicy thighs, but it's the tiny patch of fabric concealing her womanhood that I can't stop looking at. The ardor I'm feeling towards her has my skin warming. It will take a lot to cool me down.

"You are absolutely beautiful."

Her eyes fill with passion when she looks at me, tongue flicking out as she licks her kissable lips. "Your turn to shed some clothes."

I've realized that Amore isn't one of those women that hides behind fake sensibilities. She seems to speak her mind, and gets straight to the point, which is something I appreciate. I don't like falseness in any shape or form.

As I pull my jacket off, Amore pushes herself onto her elbows, watching me as I undress. Her eyes follow each movement until I am standing before her naked. Every flicker of her gaze is like a stroke of her fingers. Moving between her legs I place my hands on her upper thighs pulling her closer. Her head drops to the bed as I slide my hands down her stocking covered legs to her knees. Lifting her legs up, I lean down, kissing my way up one perfect leg. Her hand lifts to my shoulder as I kiss and nibble my way up towards her heated womanhood.

When I am but a breath away from her center, , I slide to the other leg, kissing and nibbling my way up that one as well. I hear her groan in frustration, which has me smiling. My dear wife is not a patient person.

"Gino!"

She gasps when I bite her inner thigh, just as my fingers loosen the fastenings on her stockings. Sliding my hands to the thin string of silk holding up her panties on each side, I tug. The fabric seems to disintegrate under my strength as it comes apart in my hands.

Gliding my hands up her body, I slip my fingers inside the top of her lingerie. Her torso lifts like a cat stretching in pleasure. Pulling sharply, I expose her breasts. Her nipples pebble when the cool air touches them.

This woman before me was clearly made to be loved—made to be worshiped. Her body is what erotic fantasy befalls most men, absolute decadence.

Moving up her body, I take a nipple between my lips, licking, kissing, and nibbling, driving us both mindless with passion.

"Gino," Amore murmurs as I lower my one hand to her heated sex, moving my finger over her swollen nub. Her fingers entwine in my hair as she holds me against her breasts. Her hold is tight, hips moving against my fingers as I stroke her with a determined rhythm.

"Gino, oh, ohh." When I sense her climax at a peaking point, I take both her wrists in one of my hands, pulling them above her head and position myself so I can enter her. We both gasp in pleasure when we are fully joined.

"Mine. You are now mine," I say as I lift my head to look deep into her glazed, passion-filled eyes.

"Like you are mine," she states with such conviction that I can't help but smile.

All thoughts race out of my mind when Amore moves her hips, making me close my eyes and groan in deep pleasure. Fuck, this woman is dangerous. With her sexy body, she's like a dormant volcano at the peak of erupting.

I start to move my hips, my lips moving over hers, kissing her with the same fervent rhythm of our bodies.

My body is about to explode in ecstasy, but I hold on until I feel Amore stiffening under me, her muscles tensing around me, gripping me tight within her body.

"Gi… nooo!" Amore screams as she orgasms.

I let go of my tight control, roaring my release deep within her body. I usually pull out, but she is my wife and one day hopefully the mother of my children. There is no reason to be careful about procreating.

I don't know what Amore's thoughts are on having children, but sooner or later I would like to have some. I'm not in a hurry, but I'm not going to hold back anymore because Amore will be the one to give me a family.

"Well… we won't… have any problems there," Amore quips breathlessly.

Sliding out, I lay down next to Amore, pulling her into my arms.

"I know that we have challenges ahead of us, but I think we are off to a good start."

Amore's statement has me grunting. That is an understatement. We are two main pawns from two different crime famiglias. I am sure the challenges will be intense, but the moment I accepted this union, I took on those challenges, and as such, I will do the best I can to make our marriage a real one.

"If you are always honest with me, then everything will go well," I warn.

"You too, Gino, we need to make this work, we need to bring peace to the Capella and the Nessun Perdone." I can hear the conviction in her voice, the passion of bringing peace into her life fills her soul.

"Was this union all because of Matteo?"

She stiffens, but I feel her nod.

"You think he's powerful enough to take down the Nessun Perdone?"

"Matteo has been recruiting ever since his father died. He has confronted us directly, which means that he's feeling like he's powerful enough to win," she informs me.

"Well, now he will have to face the Capella Famiglia too if he wants to rise to the top."

Amore raises her head from my chest, her eyes clashing with mine. "You will join our fight?"

Her question has me raise a brow. "No."

She looks shocked and angry.

"I won't join your fight, but I will protect you against anyone that deems to hurt you or your family."

Her angry expression changes to one of acceptance.

"That's fair," she murmurs, laying her head down again. Her fingers stroke my chest as she slowly nods off to sleep. I still can't believe that this woman in my arms is now my wife. A strong determined woman that will stand against all odds to protect her family, a woman that has given me more passion in one night than I have ever felt in my life. A woman that will keep me on my toes, and I'm sure will fight with me at every turn, but she has ignited excitement in my life—an excitement that I thought I would never feel again, and I haven't felt since the death of my family.

Looking down at the top of her head on my chest, I smile. Today is the beginning of an unsure future, but a future that I am looking forward to.

AMORE 5

It has been a month since our wedding day and even though everything started wonderfully, and the passion we feel for each other drives us every night to seek out each other's company, the outside threats are starting to penetrate our bubble. Worry and different views are starting to intrude and ignite fights between us.

When Matteo found out that we had united the two famiglias he made a couple of nasty threats, but that was the end of it, or so we thought. Yesterday I received a message to meet with Matteo, when telling Gino, let's just say he didn't take it too well.

An argument started with him thinking that he could tell me not to meet Matteo. I am my own woman and I have always done what I wanted when I wanted, and there's not an overprotective male that is going to stop me now.

If I think about it, it's endearing that he wants to keep me safe, but I have never been the sit back and see what happens type of person. Instead, I'm always the one in the front-line charging.

Gino left this morning in a rage, promising mayhem on Matteo for contacting me. I left him to his ranting as I organized my meeting with Matteo. I know that I can't trust him, that he more than likely has some plan up his sleeve in wanting to meet me. Well, if he thinks that he can get what he wants by convincing me to his misdeeds, he will be disappointed.

"Are you going out, Amore?" Looking up from my phone, I see Teresa looking at me from the doorway to the kitchen.

"Morning, Teresa." Teresa is great, she is like a loving aunt. She's a genuine, caring woman that has shown herself to be loyal to Gino and now me. I have no doubts that she will do anything in her power for our wellbeing. "Yes, but I will be back in time for dinner."

"What should I tell Gino if he phones?" I frown at her question; he will not be pleased to know that I ignored his warning and went to meet Matteo after all.

"Tell him I went out, if he wants to talk to me, he can phone me."

"Amore, you catch more with honey than vinegar. Keep that in mind, it has worked well for me." With those words, she turns back into the kitchen, continuing with what she was doing. Walking after her, I stop at the door, seeing her by the sink about to turn on the tap.

"What do you mean?"

She glances back at me and then turns to face me. "In a marriage, it's always difficult at first to find a balance when accepting each other. If a woman wants her man to agree with her, she does not fight him all the time. She uses sweet words and loving gestures to get her way." She approaches until she is standing a step away from me.

Lifting her hand, she strokes my cheek. "You are an intelligent, strong woman, you don't have to do things alone. Now you have a man to help you, and that you can help. Working together, the two of you can accomplish anything you want."

Placing my hand over hers, I shake my head in bemusement. "How did you become so wise?"

She laughs in amusement. "Age," she quips with a wink.

"You're not that old, Teresa," I say with a smile, and then take a step forward to hug her close. "Thank you." From the minute I walked into this house, Teresa has made me feel at home—made me feel like I belong. Being away from Papa and Leo for the first time, I would have been homesick if it wasn't for Teresa's welcoming presence.

"Now, I better get on with my chores, they don't get done by themselves."

"Are you sure you don't want us to get someone to help you?" I know that Gino has offered before and Teresa has been adamant about doing everything herself, but this is a big house and she really doesn't have to do everything alone.

"No, I like doing everything my way. I don't want some young girl fluffing around."

I shake my head, grinning. "Well, I need to go. See you later." Turning, I make my way out of the house and towards where my car is parked. What Teresa said made sense, I know that Gino will be livid if he finds out that I met with Matteo. Therefore, what better way to make it right then to invite Gino to join us. I know that he won't like it, but at least he will know that I'm not going behind his back to meet with him.

From experience, I know that men in the mafia are naturally suspicious. If I had to do this without telling him, he would take it as a direct challenge. Teresa is right in what she said, the best way to deal with Gino is not the confrontational way, because he is a warrior, he will not back down from a fight, and because I won't either, the best way forward is to convince him that I'm complying with his wishes.

Making my way towards my offices, I glance in the rear-view mirror to see the car with Gino's men following me. From the day that we married, he has insisted on always having two bodyguards with me. I started to argue, but he convinced me that if anything happened to me when under his responsibility, it would be a sure way to start a war between Papa and him. Knowing that he spoke the truth, I conceded. Pulling up outside Santiago's and Son shipping company, I stop the car and look up at the impressive building. Papa has various businesses which he uses as fronts for his other business.

I run Santiago's and Son shipping company and a few of his other smaller businesses, and I run them well. Papa taught Leo and me everything he knows, then when the time came, he divided his businesses and let us run them in any way we thought best.

Even though Leo is the next in line to take Papa's place as the El Padrinho, Papa made sure that we worked together in everything. He always says that Nessun Perdone is only as strong as its famiglia, and that starts with the two of us.

Leo and I fight like brother and sister, but we love each other. We understand and respect each other. Stepping out of the car, I make my way inside greeting staff as I head to my office. When I'm finally sitting behind my desk, I lean forward to place a call to Gino.

The phone rings twice before he picks up. "Amore, is everything okay?" I have never phoned Gino, he usually phones me during the day to ask if everything is okay, so for me to be phoning him out of the blue is clearly surprising him.

"Matteo is coming to Santiago's at two, I would like you to be here with me to hear what he has to say."

There is silence for a couple of seconds before I hear Gino sigh. "Does he know I am going to be there?"

"No, he asked to see me, but you are my husband, so you have every right to know what he wants."

"I will be there."

I smile at his answer and over his next words.

"Don't think I don't know what you are doing, you won't always get your way, you know?" The amusement in his voice tells me that he is pleased that I took this route.

"I have no idea what you are talking about," I quip, just as I hear a man say something. I must have caught Gino busy with business.

"I have to go; I will be there at two."

Maybe Teresa was right after all, I like to be the master of my own destiny, but maybe my destiny will be easier with the help of Gino.

There is a knock on the door and then Kim is opening it. "Your appointment for nine is here."

"Thank you, I will be with him shortly." When Kim leaves, I pick up my diary, adjust my silk vest, and straighten my slacks before making my way into the boardroom.

The day turns out to be one thing after another, and soon it is nearly time to meet with Matteo. Knowing what a little snake he is, I prepare myself for a verbal fight of wits. He will try something; of that I have no doubt.

When my office door opens, I look up from my laptop expecting to see Kim, only to see Gino step inside. My eyes travel over his masculine perfection in a charcoal suit.

His eyes are watchful as he glances around. "Gino, you are early." I pull my chair back and stand to walk around my desk as he approaches.

"I wanted to be here when he arrives." He stretches out his hand, his fingers stroking down the side of my torso, and then his hand snaps around my waist and he is pulling me hard against him.

"I don't like you being placed in danger." His statement comes out like a growl before he lowers his head and takes my lips in a blistering kiss that leaves no doubt in my mind of his intentions. His other hand grabs my ass cheek as he holds me in place while his body rubs against me with passion.

Gino's touch is like an aphrodisiac, it has everything leaving my mind, and only his touch and his kisses remain. I can feel his hardness against me, teasing me, provoking me. When he finally lifts his head, we are both ready to tear each other's clothes off.

"You make me forget everything around me, that is dangerous." His confession has my heart racing. To know I have the same reaction on Gino that he has on me is heart-warming.

When getting together like we did, there's always uncertainty of how a relationship will progress, but besides the difference in opinion, we actually get along really well. We have more in common than I would have ever suspected, and Gino is a considerate, understanding man.

He is a strong, no nonsense kind of person. He likes it straight with no hidden agendas and to be honest, so do I. I have decided to give my all to this relationship because I realize that we can be amazing together. Not just physically, but in every other sense, too.

I lift my hand to touch his stubbled cheek. His magnetic eyes following my every move. His dark hair gleams in the light from outside. Gino is a handsome man, and when he walks into a room, he has women turning their heads to admire him, and men looking at him wanting to be him.

"Maybe tonight..."

His words are interrupted by Kim popping her head around the door to tell us that Matteo is here. I see Gino's whole countenance change. Gone is the caring lover before me and in his place is a deadly no nonsense man that exudes danger.

"I want you to be on your guard and stay behind me."

I huff. "There's no way I'm hiding behind you like a frightened woman."

Gino looks at me, his eyes hard and unrelenting. "You will listen to me. He is dangerous. I will not have you hurt; you are too important."

I feel a knot in my stomach. Did he just say I was too important to him? Is Gino feeling the same depth of caring love for me that I'm feeling for him?

"You suck at romance; do you know that?" I mutter as we start making our way towards where Matteo is waiting. Gino's hand is low on my back, guiding me towards the boardroom.

"I never professed to be romantic," he says just as we reach the boardroom.

Taking in a deep breath, I open the door and step in. "Matteo," I greet.

His eyes harden when he sees Gino stepping in behind me. "I didn't know this was going to be a party, or I would have brought champagne," he comments sarcastically.

"You wanted to meet. You didn't stipulate you wanted to meet alone," I state.

"Would you have met me alone?"

His question has me shaking my head. "No, I wouldn't."

He scowls.

"Now, what can I do for you?"

He points between Gino and me. "This marriage the two of you came up with, it won't stop me."

I can feel Gino stiffening beside me, his hand tightening on my waist.

"And what would that be, Matteo? Stop you from what?"

Matteo hasn't openly challenged the Capella Famiglia only the Nessun Perdone. He knows that he's not powerful enough to go against them.

Matteo points at me. "The Nessun Perdone knew that they didn't have a chance against me, so they thought that joining the two famiglias would stop me." He stands, his body tense as he turns to us, face red with anger. "This was your idea—a woman playing a man's game."

"What frustrates you more, Matteo? That she beat you at your own game or that she's a woman and outsmarted you?"

Gino's words have Matteo glaring at him. "You... you belittle yourself by marrying a woman that just wants to use you."

"That's my problem, not yours," Gino warns in a threatening tone.

"You don't learn, do you? Looks like losing your parents and sister wasn't enough. You need to lose your wife, too."

One minute, Gino has his hand on my back, the next he is around the table and his hands are around Matteo's neck. He pushes him back against the wall. His body vibrating with anger, his expression murderous.

"Are you threatening Amore?"

Matteo raises his arms, trying to pull Gino away, but Gino's anger is unsurmountable, it's impossible for him to break free.

Pulling Matteo forward, Gino pushes him hard against the wall again. "Are you?" he roars.

"Gino, please," I call just as the door slams open and Matteo's bodyguards rush in, followed by Gino's.

"Gino, stop!" I plead, which has him glancing at me with unfathomable pain in his eyes. I know that the murder of his family still tortures him. For Matteo to threaten to do the same to me is the worst thing he could threaten Gino with.

Matteo is now the boss to his own famiglia, killing him will bring unnecessary repercussions that we don't need.

Gino let's go, taking a step back before Matteo's men can pull him away.

"If I know that you or your famiglia had anything to do with what happened to my family, I am coming for you." Gino's words are clearly a promise, and Matteo would do well to heed them.

"You can't threaten me," Matteo gasps, still trying to catch his breath.

"That's not a threat, that's a promise. Stay away from my wife if you know what is good for your health." With those words, he turns and makes his way towards me. Taking my hand, he starts making his way out of the boardroom. "See them out," Gino says to his men.

Matteo is blustering behind us, but I don't pay him any attention. At the moment, the only thing that matters to me is to be with Gino, to ease the pain that I know must me ripping him apart.

"Where are we going?" I ask, realizing that he is guiding me out of the building and towards his car. I haven't switched off my laptop or told Kim I'm leaving but being with Gino takes precedence to everything else in that moment.

Gino doesn't reply, just helps me into the car before walking around and sliding into the driver's side. We are driving out of the parking lot and onto the highway within a few minutes. Gino is still vibrating with pent-up fury.

A few minutes later, he's turning into the cemetery, his hands fisted on the steering wheel, white with the strength he's exerting. Stopping the car near a beautiful oak tree, he glances at me. The anger is still there but not as intense, but deep sorrow is now evident in his eyes. "Will you come with me?"

I nod.

I'm guessing he wants to take me to his family's graves. What happened to his family is the essence of who Gino is today, I want to be part of his future, a balm to his past. Therefore, I will need to understand and share the pain with him.

GINO 6

The only other people that come to my family's graves are Joey, Vito, and Dom. Every year on the anniversary of their death, we all come here to pay our respects to them and promise that we are still looking and haven't given up.

Now as my wife, Amore has the right to know that side of me, to know what drives me, and what keeps me looking for their killer. Guiding Amore among the graves, we walk up to the three that have left such a gap in my life.

"I want you to know me, and to know what you have gotten yourself into by marrying me."

Amore turns and is now looking at me, her expressive eyes are sad as she places her hand on my chest, waiting for me to continue talking.

"I was up in the loft, going through some of my father's files. You see, one day when I was up there, I found clippings and files that he used to keep of things that the Capella Famiglia were involved in, notes of things that happened." I lift my hand to stroke a piece of hair away from Amore's face that has slipped out of the fastening at the back of her neck.

"I was fascinated with his life, with the Famiglia. Then that day while I was going through the files, I heard loud voices and then screaming. Instead of running down to go and help, I waited, looking through a gap in the floor that had a bird's-eye view of an area in the sitting room. Like a coward, I heard the shots, and instead of going to help and confront the killer, I hid." That is my biggest regret, the thought that I should have tried to do something, but instead I didn't do anything.

"You were only a teenager, there was nothing you could have done against a gun."

I stroke her cheek, seeing the compassion on her face. "They were my family; I should have done something." Lowering my head, I kiss her forehead. "I will never give up looking for their killer. I saw the hand of the man who murdered them. He had a tattoo between his thumb and index finger, the tattoo was of a skull and had a crow pecking at it. I will find him, and I will get revenge for what was done to them." I have dreams of the killer's hand, dreams that the hand is coming through the gap on the floor to grab me. "I will not let anything like that happen to you, if I am protective it is because I know what it's like to lose those closest to you—lose those you love."

"Do you love me?"

"I didn't want to. Loving someone can be painful, but you have wiggled yourself into my heart with your stubbornness and courage. Yes, Amore, I love you, and I promise that I will do everything in my power to keep you safe." Sliding my arms around her waist I kiss her lips. To kiss this strong-willed woman that chose me to be her husband feels right. She's a woman who can drive me crazy with exasperation, and mindless with passion, but she's also a woman that has conquered my heart, my respect and above all my loyalty. I'm truly blessed.

LOST SOUL

Warriors MC

RAINE 1

"Raine, are you sure about this?"

Glancing at Trina, I smile. Ever since confiding in Trina that I know who my mate is, and that I am meeting him tonight, she has been trying to change my mind.

"Don't worry, Trina, you know that I'm never wrong." As the Oracle, I sometimes wish that I could be wrong about certain things. I was born with an all-seeing eye for a reason, and maybe one day I will find out what that reason is, but for now, all I know is that I saw I will meet my soulmate tonight.

"But a demon, Raine?" Trina can't get over the fact that my mate is a demon. To be fair, I was also hoping that it was a mistake. Demons aren't exactly the romantic, cuddly, poet types. If anything, they are hard-hitting, killing machines. But it seems like fate has other plans for me.

"It will be fine, Trina. Trust me, I'm sure that he won't be too pleased finding out his mate is the Oracle."

"Well, at least the two of you will meet in a crowded place. I wouldn't trust a demon otherwise," Trina complains.

That's true. Even though I'm not worried that Damien is going to hurt me; I do worry about the others he travels with. Damien is part of the Warriors MC, a group of bikers that are a mixture of outcast beings. I've never actually met Damien, but he sent me a message asking for a meeting. I know he's asking for a consultation to see if I can help him find his soul.

Demons are born with no soul. Only by finding their soulmate are they able to feel and gain their full powers. Little does Damien know, I'm actually his soulmate and the only that can restore his lost soul.

I'm also feared by many. Not because I'm dangerous, but because I have knowledge that some of them would rather I not have.

Lifting my hand, I stroke my fingers through my long, auburn tresses. The silver hoops in my ears catch the light as I enter the pub. Most of the people in the pub are human and have no idea that beings like Damien exist, or people like me for that matter.

I'm the daughter of a Witch and an Elf. My mother was ruler of her coven, and when she met my father, things were shaky at first because witches don't like other beings in their home. With time, they adapted, and my father came to live in her coven.

It's not often that different factions join as mates, but it happens. And unlucky for me, I'm one of them.

Looking around, I see the pub is nearly full. The noise of the music and the patrons talking, and eating is deafening for someone with sensitive hearing.

I know Kole, the owner of Storybook Pub, he is a sweetheart. Even though I haven't seen him for quite some time, I know that he's still around helping those in need. Kole has Pub's all over the world, but I think this one in Cape Town, South Africa, is one of his favourites. I know that it's the faction's favourite pub in the area, too. Even though no one has ever mentioned anything to Kole, I think he suspects that his clientele in the Cape Town Storybook Pub aren't always what they seem.

"I don't think he's here yet," Trina says as she looks around from where she's standing next to me.

"No, I don't think he is." I did book him for an hour from now, but I wanted to make sure that I have a table that faces the door. I need to see him as soon as he walks in because even though I have seen him in a vision, it's not the same as seeing him in real life.

I usually have beings wanting to see me to help them with different problems that they might have. I have even had demons ask me to find their souls before too, but I never in a hundred years would have thought that I was a demon's salvation. A demon will only live one hundred and fifty years if he doesn't find his soul. If he finds his soul, he will turn immortal. The only way to kill a demon after his coupling is to kill his mate.

If I consent to couple with Damien, my life expectancy will also lengthen. Instead of the five or six hundred years that witches usually live, I'll be immortal unless I'm killed.

If I let Damien touch me, he will know that I'm his, and he will do everything in his power to have me accept him. That's why I can't let him touch me until I'm sure that I want this. I want to make sure that even though Damien is a demon, he isn't evil to his very core. I need to know that there is some kind of good in him.

"Hello, ladies."

Looking up, I see Greg, one of the waiters at the pub, standing next to our table. I smile. Greg is human, and a known sweet talker, but he's harmless and a real sweet guy.

"I haven't seen you around here in a while, my days have been much darker without the two of you."

I laugh, shaking my head. "Hi, Greg, does that actually work on anyone?" Trina asks with a grin.

"Made you laugh, didn't it?" he says with an exaggerated wink.

Trina is taller than me, but that isn't difficult because most people are. I'm five feet two inches and the smallest in our coven, but what I don't have in height, I have in personality, or so I like to tell myself.

"Would you like your usual?" At my nod and Trina's confirmation, he leaves to go get our drinks.

"I have missed this place," Trina says as she looks around. We used to come here as a group, but there have been problems with the werewolves, and some of the coven have been out hunting them. Therefore, we aren't supposed to be here today. It's become dangerous to be out unless we are in a group.

When Damien phoned, I first told him I couldn't meet him at the moment. But after disconnecting the call and having a vision of him, I knew I was meant to meet him. He's the man for me. We were both made for each other, and even though he's a demon and I'm the Oracle, our fate has been written. If it's meant to be, then who am I to fight against it?

"We shouldn't have come. Look who has just walked in."

I'm so distracted with my own thoughts that I don't notice Blaze walk in. His eyes are trained on the two of us as he approaches. Tin is right behind him, glaring at us with a scowl on his face.

"Great," I mumble as they come to stand before us.

"Should you ladies be out and about?" Blaze asks sarcastically. He looks around purposefully as if he's looking for someone, when we all know that he could smell everyone in this pub the minute he walked in. "Looks like you are living on the edge."

"What do you want, Blaze?" I ask with a raised brow.

"Well, if you stopped breathing, that would be great, but I doubt you are willing to accommodate us."

I smile at him—a smile that I'm sure doesn't reach my eyes.

"I'm afraid you will have a long time to wait for that." Actually, I have no idea how long I will live or not. That is one thing about being an oracle, I can't see anything about myself. That's why I have no idea if Damien and I will make a good couple or not. The only reason I saw we are mates is because of Damien wanting to find his soul. Everything to do with me is usually blocked from my view.

"You think you're so high and mighty with that little trick of yours in seeing the future. One swipe of my hand and you would be dead."

"Not until I get what I'm here for." The voice coming from behind Tin has every fibre in my being at attention.

Blaze snaps around, his eyes blazing with anger. Tin also has his back towards us as he faces the two men before him.

Both are tall, over six feet, with raven black hair. They both wearing leather biker jackets, they have an air about them that screams danger. There's an air of danger around them that warns everyone around to be cautious.

Damien is the one that spoke. His hair reaches his shoulders, and his jaw is tense as he looks at the men. His eyes are two dark orbs promising hell to anyone that dares to cross him.

"Guys, you know the rules. No fights in here." My eyes snap towards where Kole is approaching with a scowl on his face. I see the men glance towards him and then Blaze is lifting his arms.

"No problem, Kole," he says as he steps away, patting Kole on the shoulder. "See you around, Void."

I see the two demons tense at the name, but they don't move. Instead, their eyes stay glued on the two werewolves as they make their way towards a table at the back of the pub.

DAMIEN 2

Those motherfuckers are lucky they are in here or I would be showing them what a void feels like.

I turn towards Kole, he raises a brow in question which has me nodding. He then turns towards the two women before me, "I should have known the two of you would be in the middle of this," he says in a playful tone.

"Of course, who else?" One of them says.

My eyes clash with the one that is looking at me, her moss green eyes feel like they are penetrating my mind. There's no doubt that she's the Oracle, and a tiny wisp of a woman, who's gorgeous in every way. She has a tight little tank top on with a wide skirt that drops to her feet. The top does nothing to hide her luscious breasts. Her hair is long, curly, and a burnt auburn colour that has my fingers twitching to thread them through her tresses and feel if it really is as silky as it looks.

"Oracle?"

She nods. "My name is Raine." Her voice is husky, reminding me of a warm autumn day when the leaves rustle in the trees.

Her eyes don't leave mine, as places two glasses on the table, which tells me that they have been here for a little while as they have had time to order their drinks already.

"What can I get for you guys?"

"Whiskey straight up," I order.

"Same," Zen says as he takes a seat before the other woman who's sitting at the table, looking at us with disgust. He glares at her. "If we revolt you, you are more than welcome to leave.

Placing a hand on his shoulder I squeeze it in warning.

"I was here first,." The woman says sarcastically, her body tense as she glares back at Zen.

"Trina, please," Raine says in anger.

Trina looks up at Raine. I don't know what passes between the two, but Trina is lifting her hands in the air as if she's surrendering.

"I'm sorry, please don't take offense," Raine tries to appease.

Trina sighs but doesn't say anything.

"Enough of this. Let's get this over and done with and get out of here," Zen says as he looks over at me.

But for some reason I'm in no hurry to leave Raine. Something about her calls to me.

"You know why I'm here, are you able to help me?"

Zen was against this, but I'm tired of going through life feeling nothing. I want to know what it's like to feel happiness, or even pain. To be in this monotonous existence of unfeelingness, year after year has worn me down. I'm now one hundred and thirty-eight years old, and even though I still have a few years to live without finding my soul, I want to end this lonely existence of unfeeling vastness that is my life.

"You know what this entails don't you? You know that if you find your soul, you will be bound to that person for all eternity?" If she only knew how long I have waited for this. How long I've craved a touch that I could actually feel something with. To experience a sexual act and all the feelings that come with it, instead of the empty release that it's always been.

"I know."

"You're ready to live your life bound to someone else?" Her question has me raising a brow.

"I won't be the only one that is bound. This is a two-way thing."

My statement has her nodding.

"I'm telling you this is a waste of time," Zen says with a shake of his head as he takes his drink from the waiter.

"We can agree on that," Trina mutters as she takes a sip of her drink.

Ignoring both of them, I don't break eye contact as I watch Raine take in a deep breath before she nods as if to something she is thinking in her head, and then stretches out both her hands.

"Raine," Trina calls in a warning tone.

Raine glances at her and shakes her head. "No, this is how it should be," she says in a firm tone. Then, looking back at me she states, "take my hands."

I have never been around an oracle or any such person in my life. Therefore, I have no idea what I need to do for her to read my future, but I guess touching her is one of them.

Lifting my hands, I'm about to place them over hers when she pulls away, staring at my hands. "You need to take those off."

Looking at my gloved hands, I'm the one frowning now. Pulling back my hands, I remove my black motorcycle gloves, placing them on the table next to my elbow before I stretch out my hands again. This time I'm the one that turns my palms up, waiting for her much smaller hands to fit in mine.

Slowly, she once again stretches out her arms. Her hands hover over mine for a few seconds before she finally lays them gently on mine.

"Fuck," I whisper the moment her hands touch mine. It's like an explosion of emotions blasts through me. The sounds and smells all around me become more intense. Her fragrance, something close to exotic flowers and honey, surround me. My hands close over hers. The softness of her skin feels tender as a strange feeling overwhelms me—a feeling like I don't ever want to open my hands and let her go.

"You?" I ask, still unsure if she's showing me what it will be like or if this is the real thing.

"Yes, me." I can't believe that Raine is the key to my very soul, that a woman that can tell the future, a woman that is the epitome of feelings, is my mate.

"What's going on?" Zen asks in a suspicious tone, but I ignore him.

I ignore everything but the woman before me. This woman that seems so fragile, that will barely reach my neck when standing, and a strong wind could blow her away, is my mate. She's the woman that I will be coupled with for the rest of my days.

Zen stretches out his hand. His intentions are clear. He is about to pull Raine's hand away from me. I turn towards him, everything in me rebelling at the thought of him touching Raine.

"You touch her and you're dead." My voice is low—deadly. I can hear the underlying fury in my voice. Zen stops himself just before touching my woman.

"What the fuck?" he asks in confusion.

"Mine!"

Talk about not taking it well.

Zen stands, his body vibrating with tension as he looks at Damien and I. "This is a trick—some kind of magic." He turns his head to glare at Trina. "They are fucking witches. She's playing you, Brother."

"I know what I'm feeling, and I doubt anyone could restore our souls, even if for just a couple of minutes, no matter how good they are," Damien says as he continues holding my hands. Looking back at me, he inclines his head towards the outside exit door.

"I want you to come with me."

I sense Trina tensing next to me. But when we left to come here, she knew this was going to happen. Usually when we find our mates, we stay together. That will still have to be discussed between Damien and me—where we will live. But for now, we need to be together, to get to know each other and complete the bond.

Only once we consummate our union will Damien's soul be fully restored. I can feel every fibre in my body accepting this man before me. His strength vibrates through my veins like a rush of a raging river. His darkness is a pit of never-ending pain, but as soon as it filled me, it was gone like the tide had washed it away.

"Where?" I ask.

"You can't seriously be thinking about going with him, Raine!" Trina argues in outrage. "He's a demon."

"He's my mate," I state as I start to pull my hands away, but Damien holds them tighter. "Damien won't hurt me." It's silly of me to place my trust in a man that I have never met before, but deep down, I can feel that no matter what, I can trust Damien.

Standing, I finally pull my hands free. Turning to Trina, I smile when I see her worried expression. "Don't worry, I'm ready. Tell everyone I will be in touch soon."

"They're not going to like this," Trina says, but she stands and hugs me close. "Take care, Raine, and be careful," she whispers against my ear.

Turning, I come face to chest with Damien. He is standing right behind me. The scent of leather surrounds me. His biker's jacket looks well-worn and comfortable. His muscular arm comes around my shoulders as he starts to turn to guide me out of the pub.

"Well, isn't this just cosy? Maybe I should have tried my luck..."

One minute Damien's arm is around me, the next he has his hand around Blaze's throat, holding him against the wall. His dark angel portraying the danger that can be unleased from him. "Have you got a problem?" His voice is low, guttural, and every word is dripping with anger.

Demons are the perfect killers because they have no feelings to impede them. Even though Damien has found me, we are still not mated. Therefore, his possessive instincts are going to be more acute now.

Demons are possessive creatures; they will protect their mate above everything else. Blaze chose the wrong woman to pick on.

I can see Blaze's eyes start to shine a goldish colour, showing how close he is to changing. If I don't stop this soon, the humans in the pub will finally find out that there are dark things out there that they had no idea existed.

"Damien, let him go. He's not worth it." I place my hand on his arm, stroking it gently, trying to appease the fury racing through him. He turns his head towards me, his dark eyes snapping with anger. "Has he been harassing you?"

"No. The coven and wolves are not seeing eye to eye at the moment. It's not directed at me specifically." His eyes turn back towards Blaze who has now raised his hand and is pulling at Damien's tight hold.

"You ever come near my woman again and I won't stop." He lets go of Blaze's neck only to have Blaze throw a punch that Damien deflects.

"Get out," Kole warns from next to me. "I will not tolerate fighting in here."

Blaze growls low in his throat, but Damien steps back. His eyes still glowing with anger as he comes to stand in front of me. He places one hand behind him to pull me up tight against his back. His stance protective as he faces Blaze.

"We are leaving," Damien warns as he starts making his way out, constantly keeping me behind him for my safety. I see that Zen has taken it upon himself to protect Trina too, who I notice is glaring up at him, but not complaining.

When we get outside, I pull back to start making my way towards the car, but Damien pulls me back. "You ride with me," he states as he glances behind us with a frown.

"But I don't have a helmet." It's not just that. I have never been on a motorcycle, either. The thought of speeding on something that has no protection whatsoever has always frightened me.

"You can use mine."

"But what about my car?" it might not be all that fancy to look at, but I love my Mini. It's a bright cherry red with a black stipe on the right leading from the front of the hood, all the way to the back.

"One of the guys will pick it up." I'm guessing Damien is referring to one of the guys in his MC. Seeing as I have no more excuses, I nod as I let him help me with the helmet.

Damien gets on and then he's giving me a hand to help me on. "Tuck you skirt between your legs. Don't let it drag behind you." If I had known that I was going to be on a Harley today, I would have made sure to wear something more appropriate, but this will have to do for now.

I made sure to pack some clothes just in case this happened, but they are in a travel bag in my car. Tucking the skirt tight under my thighs, I place my hands on Damien's waist as he starts the bike, but before he starts riding, he takes hold of my wrists and pulls me closer to his back as he brings my arms around his waist.

His leather jacket feels soft to the touch as my hands lay against it. We start making our way just as I see Blaze and Tin walk out of the pub. Their eyes follow us as we ride past, hatred evident in their stares.

Glancing behind me, I see Zen has turned off with Trina riding behind him. It's good that he's taking her home because I was worried that somehow the Werewolves would go after her, seeing as they couldn't get hold of me.

I don't know how long we are riding before we stop in front of some high metal gates. A few seconds later, the gates are opening, and we're riding through the gates up to a three-story building. Harleys are parked in front; music is blaring and there is laughter coming from inside.

Damien helps me off the bike and then he's pulling off my helmet and placing it on the handlebars of his Harley. "These guys can be rough around the edges, but knowing you are my mate they will protect you if I'm not around," Damien says as he raises his hand to my cheek.

"Are they all demons?" I ask, slightly apprehensive to be in a demon's domain.

Damien suddenly lifts both his hands, placing one on each side of my cheeks as he looks deeply into my eyes.

"Don't be afraid, I will protect you." And then he is lowering his head, his lips touching mine. As expected, the touch of his lips on mine has a ripple tingling down my back. Lifting my arms, I slide my hands around his neck as the kiss deepens.

My body feels like it's on fire, every sense and cell vibrates with passion. I may not know Damien yet, but my body and my senses seem to know him to my very core.

DAMIEN 4

I hear steps approaching, which immediately has my demon raising. A protective instinct that I've never had before overwhelms me. In the blink of an eye, I have Raine standing behind me as I press my blade to Seth's throat. A deep growl escapes Seth, but he doesn't move. Instead, he raises his hands in surrender.

Seth is a Dragon shifter—a mean son of a bitch, but he's been a friend since we were kids. I know that Seth would do nothing to hurt my mate, but this instinct in me is stronger than my beliefs.

"What the fuck, Brother?" Seth growls deep under his breath.

I take the dagger away from his neck, but I keep Raine behind me. "You should know better than to creep up behind me." I grunt angrily at the interruption.

"Creep?" Seth asks in surprise. "Fuck, if I had been making any more noise, a deaf man would hear me." Seth inclines his head towards behind me. "Now why the fuck are you so jumpy?"

Grunting, I turn slightly to place my arm around Raine's shoulders. "Seth, meet my mate, Raine." This whole feeling thing has everything coming at me at once. When

Seth looks at Raine, I want to skin him for even looking at her. Son of a bitch, I need to get my woman to myself for a very long time before I introduce her to anyone else because I swear if anyone even thinks to approach her, I will kill them.

Seth's surprised look has me guiding Raine around him and towards the back door of the Warriors MC. I can hear Seth mumbling from behind us, but for now, I'm just interested in getting my woman to my room.

Opening the back door, I can hear men in the front talking and laughing. I want to get to my room without anyone else stopping us. I will have more than enough time later to introduce Raine and let everyone know that I have found my mate.

"Are you hiding me?"

Raine's question has me stopping with my hand on the bedroom door. "No, I just don't want to introduce you right now. I have all these feelings coming at me—things that I have no idea what to do with." One thing that no one knows about us is that when demons mate, they also come into their full power. Once mated my full strength will fill me, and I will finally feel complete. At the moment, I'm feeling all these sensations overwhelming me, filling me with confusion because I have no idea what I'm feeling. But one thing I do know, is that this woman before me is my mate, and I will do anything in my power to keep her safe.

Raine is looking up at me, her beautiful eyes seem to be penetrating my every thought. "We will work through this together." I have always been one to walk alone, my only family has been the men in the Warriors MC, I don't know how to share my life or even how to accept the help of others.

Opening the door to my room, I wait for Raine to walk in before I close the door behind me. I see Raine looking around. Now that I have a mate, I look around my sparse room as I try to see what Raine is seeing. The only things in my room are my double bed pulled up against the wall, a chest of draws where I keep my T-shirts and jeans and a single chair against the wall.

"You can get whatever you want for the room?" Raine glances over her shoulder at me, there's a surprised look on her face.

"You want us to live here?"

"Yes, where else?"

I don't have a house anywhere else, even though I have more than enough money to keep us comfortable for a long time to come without worrying about anything. This is my home.

"I have always lived at the coven." Does she expect me to live with a bunch of cranky witches? I would kill them by the end of the first day. Snaking my arm around her waist, I pull her hard against me. Enough talk. Her much smaller body fits me perfectly. The top of her head just reaches my chest.

"You're mine." I grunt just before I take her lips in a possessive kiss—a kiss that leaves our hearts racing in anticipation. Drawing my hands under her arms, I pick her up. The way her passion-filled eyes are looking at me with such trust, fills me with such tenderness—a sensation that I have never had before. Her head lowers as she combs her fingers through my hair. Her legs slide around my waist, her womanhood rubbing against my cock. The passion races through my body like a river of lava looking for release.

"Damien." My name being whispered is like a ray of light penetrating a mist of darkness that I have lived with my whole life. I start kissing down her fragile neck, hearing her murmur of pleasure as I nip and then lick it gently. Never have I wanted to please a woman as much as I want to please my mate. Never have I cared about anyone else like I now care about this woman in my arms.

"I want you," I growl, feeling my self-control starting to slip. I need to make this woman mine, in every sense of the word. I can feel the urgency pushing me to take her—to bind her to me for all eternity.

I left finding my mate until later in life because I just didn't want to be responsible for another being. But lately, I have wanted more. I've wanted to know what it's like to actually feel and to have my full power. Even though I've never really had a woman I wanted to hang on to, what I'm feeling now has me wanting to tie her to me.

Taking in a breath, I can smell her essence, a smell that I will hold deep within me, a smell that I will be able to find anywhere. Walking towards the bed, I lower her. My fingers slide into the hem of her skirt. As she lays back, I stand, pulling the skirt off as I move. Each inch of skin that's revealed to me is like a beacon calling me. Her tiny black panties barely covering her honeypot.

Raine looks at me, her expression is one of pure lust. Her eyes are filled with a fiery passion that promises heaven in her arms. Her eyes never leave me as she pulls her tank top off, her breasts bouncing in relief at their sudden release from the confinement of the built-in bra on her top.

Her rosy, pink nipples pebble with the cooler air, calling for my touch, my mouth, and my kisses. She lays before me in all her glory. The only thing covering her is the tiny black patch of her panties. Grabbing my T-shirt, I pull it off in one swipe. I hear her gasp when she sees the scar that crosses the length of my chest.

Even though my chest is tattooed, the scar is still visible. "What happened?" she whispers as she sits up.

"The fucker that wanted to see my insides is now rotting in hell, and I'm still here breathing. That's all that there is to it."

That fucker was my father, but there's no way that I'm going to tell her that. At least, not at this very moment. I have more important things to think about.

"I'm so sorry." The fact that I hear the sincerity in her voice has me pausing as I throw my jeans towards the chair, now standing before her completely naked.

"Don't be. It taught me a valuable lesson." A lesson never to trust no one, no matter who they are. That lesson has kept me alive this long.

Placing my knee on the bed, I bend forward to take her lips. Her sweetness is intoxicating—penetrating. Sliding my fingers in her hair, I turn her head up so that I can kiss her thoroughly and completely. My woman will know who she belongs to—who will protect her no matter what.

Her hands move over my torso and down my tattooed chest as I kiss her. Her sexy murmurs have me as hard as fucking steel.

 Pushing her back against the mattress, I run my eyes over the perfection that is my woman. Her body is a sculpture of perfection. Running my hands up her torso, I cup her rounded breasts. Their size fits my palm perfectly, as if they were made for them. I move to kiss them. She raises her legs to fold them around my waist, holding me closer to her as I worship her body. I can feel her hands on my shoulders, stroking, kneading, and making me feel wanted. Things that I have never felt before.

"Damien, don't make me wait." Her voice is breathless. Her lips slightly parted and red from our kisses. "Not today."

As a demon, the sexual act has always been about release and nothing else. But today with Raine, the unexplainable drive to pleasure her—to touch her, is making me feel stronger and more fulfilled than any release I have ever had in my hundred odd years.

Standing, I grab her knees, pulling her to the edge of the bed. She gasps at the sudden movement, but that is nothing like the cry of pleasure leaving her lips a second later when I plunge deep into her body.

Everything around me seems to still. My senses increase a thousand percent as I feel Raine's heart beating as if it's my own. I can hear every one of her breaths deep within me, feel her blood coursing through her veins as if it's rushing through my own veins. Pulling slightly out, I once again plunge into her. Her pleasure becomes my pleasure, her cries driving me. I thrust, retreat, thrust, retreat, watching my woman's every expression as her eyes never leave mine.

For the first time in my life, I feel my heart racing. It's a tenderness that I'm sure a demon has no place feeling, and it fills me completely. Then Raine's muscles are tightening around me, her gasps get louder as her hands fist the sheet. "Oh, ohh, Dami... onnn," she cries as she is thrown over the edge of pleasure.

I can't hold back any longer, her muscles milk my orgasm with a vengeance that has me roaring my release for all to hear, "Mine!"

RAINE 5

Everyone knows that sex with a mate is like nothing ever felt before, but I never, for the life of me, thought it would have been earth shattering like it was.

Damien is nothing like I expected. Yes, he's a dominant through and through, but he's tender and caring. Something that I would never have thought to find in a demon. I know that all the feelings are overwhelming him because he seems to not know what to do with them. But one thing about him is that he isn't fighting it. Instead, he's riding the wave of each feeling and sensation as it fills him, trying them all out.

We spent most of the night making love. Damien made sure to couple with me thoroughly. There will be no doubt who I belong to. I know that being from two different factions there will be fighting until we become accustomed to each other. But I also know that because we are fated to be together, we will overcome whatever obstacle is thrown at us, and we'll rise above it stronger than before.

Looking around, I frown. This room really needs some colour, and something to soften it up. Currently, it's impersonal and cold. Even though Damien will never be a fuzzy, warm-hearted demon, he will at least be more sensitive to things around him.

I don't know how long I've been sleeping, but after waking up about half an hour ago, I slipped into the shower, which I was happy to find Damien had in his room. I wasn't looking forward to walking around the club looking for a bathroom. It doesn't seem like my clothes have made their way here yet, so I put on one of Damien's T-shirts, knotting it at my waist, then pull my skirt on.

I will have to go commando until I get my clothes, but with the long skirt, it doesn't matter because no one will see. Damien was already gone when I woke up, and even though I would have rather woken up next to him, it has given me time to shower and get dressed. Because with the way my mate was during the night, I'm sure we wouldn't be doing much more than lying in bed again today if I continued to stay in bed.

Taking in a deep breath, I walk towards the door. I don't know what to expect from the men here at the club, but I have heard stories about the Warrior MC; they are not to be trifled with. I know that factions usually pay the MC to help them with difficult situations with other beings because they are hardened men that are also warriors. Men who have, for one reason or another, been banned from their own factions.

I make my way down a much quieter corridor, hoping that I'm going the right way. I'm nearly at the end when a mountain of a man covers the entrance. His eyes travel over every inch of my body.

Maybe this was a bad idea.

"You must be Raine!"

Well, at least he knows who I am.

"Yes, and you are?"

Suddenly he grins, his arms crossing over his chest. Impressive muscular arms that will destroy a man with a simple swoop. "Curious?"

I find myself raising a brow at his question.

"Are you really an Oracle?"

I nod.

"How does this whole Oracle thing work?"

Shrugging, I take a step closer. "I usually help people with issues they might have. Sometimes I can see what's going to happen in the future."

"What's going to happen to me?"

"If you don't get out of my way, you're going to be bashed over the head."

Damien's words have me grinning as the man glances over his shoulder.

"Stop being so grumpy," the man says as he steps forward to let Damien pass. Damien's eyes clash with mine, and everything that happened the night before flashes through my mind. I can feel my cheeks flushing with heat as I can see by the way his eyes are looking at me, he is thinking about the same thing.

"I woke up, and you were gone," I murmur as he slides his hands around my waist, pulling me against him.

"We had a meeting this morning. I wanted to let everyone know about you." He inclines his head towards the other man when he talks about the meeting, which tells me how the man knew my name.

"I see you have met, Tork."

Looking over at the other man, I see him looking at me curiously.

"Actually, Tork hadn't introduced himself yet." By the way Tork's eyes shine a honey colour, I can tell that he's a Bear shifter, and from the looks of him, a curious one at that. "Nice to meet you, Tork."

"Welcome to the family, Oracle," Tork says in a deep voice. "I still want to know all about how it works." And with those words, he turns, leaving Damien shaking his head.

"You will find that Tork analyses everything. He sucks up knowledge like a sponge."

I smile. You would never have guessed that from the man that was standing before me just moments ago. Anyone meeting him on the road would only see a dangerous biker, instead of the curious man.

"I was coming to get you for breakfast, but I must warn you, everyone is dying to meet you, so be prepared." He places his index finger under my jaw as he kisses me tenderly.

I feel such a deep connection with this man that I have just met—a connection that I've never felt with anyone before. Looking at Damien in the light of day, I see the powerful, good looking man that is my mate.

His raven dark hair touches his wide shoulders. His dark, penetrating look reminds me of the amazing night we both shared—the night that transformed both of our lives. Damien is now my mate, and as such, the most important part of me. As the oracle, I come across various beings and the things that I see sometimes aren't the happiest. Beings aren't always satisfied with what I tell them. Damien knows nothing of my life or the danger that I am sometimes placed in because of it.

I have no doubt that he will keep me safe from everything and everyone out there. I know that he's a warrior, and that being part of the Warriors MC brings with it a lot of shady business.

"Come, Baby girl, let's go face the music." Sliding his arm around my waist, Damien guides me through the door and towards a room full of imposing men.

DAMIEN 6

The seven men before us have been with me through thick and thin. I trust them with my life, but I seem to keep the trust of my mate only to myself because I find myself reluctant to introduce her to the others.

They have all stopped talking and are now standing, facing us. "Raine, I want you to meet, Xent, our very own Vampire and lord of the night."

Xent is leaning against the far wall, seeming to be nearly asleep. But knowing Xent, he is taking everything in and is aware of everything around him. Xent nods his head; his light grey eyes catch mine and I can see the approval in them.

"Over there is, Seth; you met him last night." Seth grins at Raine, taking a step towards us, but he stops when I growl low in my throat. No matter how much I trust these men, I don't want them near my woman.

"Fuck, Damien, I'm not going to take a bite out of her, you know?" Seth mutters as he throws up his hands.

"You don't need to come near her, either."

"Are you fucking serious?" Seth asks with raised brows.

"It's his mate. He's still feeling protective over her. Give him space," Tork states from where he took a seat.

"I'm standing right here, you know?" I growl, which has Tork showing me the finger just as Veron places his hand on Tork's shoulder, grinning.

"Standing with Tork is Veron." Veron nods at Raine, but he doesn't try to approach. "Veron doesn't talk." I won't go into details about any of the guys here right now with Raine, or the reason for them being here. Being a Phoenix was not easy for Veron growing up. It's a past that he would rather forget — a past that none of us bring up. I can feel Raine stiffening under my hand. I suspect that she's afraid of being confronted by so many outlaw men, but she will soon realize that I will never let anything happen to her. And these men I'm introducing her to will also be her friends.

"This here is, Zev." I point towards our very own werewolf and the best tracker in all of Cape Town.

"Welcome, beautiful!"

Zev's greeting has me grunting in anger. I know that Zev means nothing by his greeting, but I don't like other men noticing that my woman is beautiful.

"And Zen you already know." Zen is sitting on one of the chairs looking on at everything with a bored expression on his face. He's also a demon and the closest to me of all the men here.

"Dude, is your woman's eyes supposed to do that?" Seth asks as he stares at Raine with a frown.

Looking down at Raine, I turn her gently towards me only to see her eyes clouded over with a milky colour. It is clear that she's having a vision, or whatever oracles do.

"Fuck," I whisper in anger at myself. How am I supposed to help my woman if I don't know what the fuck

I'm helping her with? Should I shake her or give her water? Looking up, I see all the men looking at her with different expressions on their faces.

"What the fuck am I supposed to do?" I have never been one to be unsure or feel so helpless, but this situation has me wanting to roar my anger at seeing her like this and not knowing what to do to help her. The vision is clearly not a good one as her breathing is laboured and her complexion has paled.

I place my hands on her upper arms only to have a tremor race through her whole body as if it's an electric shock.

"I don't think you should try to wake her," Tork says

"She's not sleeping," Zev says in exasperation.

Suddenly, Raine's haunted voice has all of us stiffening. "Trouble is coming…" Her eyes are still murky, and her body tense with whatever she is experiencing. "Brace yourselves. A beauty so great, you will encounter, but evil lurks to attack from the most unlikely source. Be aware. Be aware, with mother nature, she a life will try to spare."

Raine unexpectedly starts to fall. If my hands weren't on her upper arms, my woman would've fallen on the ground.

"Raine?" I can feel my heart racing. For the first time in my life, I fear. I fear that my woman is in pain and that I won't be able to help her. I can hear her heart beating as I hold her tight against me. Her complexion still deathly pale. Her eyes now closed.

If this is what she goes through every time she has a vision, then fuck that. I will insist that she stop having them immediately.

"Raine?" I kiss her forehead tenderly, feeling the knot in my stomach tighten more and more with each minute that passes and my woman doesn't open her eyes.

"Maybe lay her down?" Seth suggests as he points to the table that we usually sit around for our meetings. As I start making my way towards the table, Raine opens her eyes, a dazed look is in them, but at least it's my mate once again.

"Raine?"

Her eyes capture mine as she focuses on me. "Sorry, that one..." Her voice breaks, sounding dry. "Came unexpectedly."

"Tork, water!" I call as I take a seat on one of the chairs. Instead of laying her on the table, I sit her on my lap, wanting to have her as close to me as possible. A glass of water is thrust at me. Taking it from a concerned looking Tork, I place it at her lips.

"Does that happen often?" Xent asks, now standing with the others around us.

After drinking a few sips of water, Raine shakes her head. "Usually, I know it's coming and have a chance to prepare, but this one just hit me," she says as she looks around at all the men.

"What did you mean?" Zen asks.

"I don't know. All I know is that danger is coming, and you must be cautious. It will attack when you least expect it."

"So basically, like everything else in our lives," Zev says with a shrug.

"But she said a beauty so great we will encounter. What beauty is that?" Tork asks. "Does it mean we will meet a beautiful woman and she will be the danger?"

"I'm sorry, sometimes my visions are clear, and sometimes they are just warnings, like in this case." I can feel the regret in Raine's voice for not being able to answer the men as they would like.

"Enough!" I will not have my woman feeling bad for something she has no control over. "She has warned us. It is more than we had before." The men know my anger. They know when not to push me, and this is one of those times.

"Well, it sure is interesting." Trust Tork to think so. I'm sure he's going to analyse the warning to exhaustion and come back with every possible option. A plate is suddenly thrust at me. Looking up, I see Veron. He has a concerned look on his face as he inclines his head towards Raine.

"Thanks, Brother." With everything that happened, I completely forgot that I was going to feed my woman. Looking at the plate, I see that Veron added everything to it. I hope she likes variety. There's toast, scrambled eggs, sausage, mushrooms, cheese, and even a peach. "I promised you breakfast," I say, bringing the plate closer for her to see.

"Oh, umm." Her eyes widen as she looks at the plate. "Thank you so much. This is really nice." Sitting up, she looks at all the men. I see her cheeks brighten with colour. Is Raine embarrassed?

"Sorry about what happened. I promise you it doesn't happen that often."

I realize Raine is feeling self-conscious.

"I thought you guys were hungry?" I ask with a pointed look at the food on the table. They take the hint and start scrambling to fill their plates with breakfast. Raine makes like she's going to stand, but I hold her in place. Looking down at her, I raise my brow, wondering where she thinks she's going.

"Is there a reason why I can't sit in my own chair?" she asks softly, but everyone hears. Even though the others will be teasing me for days, I don't give a fuck.

"Yes. It's because of what happened earlier. I didn't like that feeling of not being able to help you." Just talking about it has my anger rising. "You could fall and hurt yourself, so for now you stay close to me until I know how to keep you safe."

My confession has a beaming smile lighting up her face. She looks at me with such happiness that I suddenly feel like the luckiest guy alive.

"You're so sweet." Her words have some guys choking on their laughter. This seals my fate. They will never let me live this down, but I don't give a fuck. I would have her call me sweet as often as she wants if it puts that smile on her face.

"You don't need to worry; I have been having these visions since I was a little girl."

"I don't like it. How do I help you?"

Raine lifts her hand to my cheek. Sitting up, she kisses my lips, ignoring the others watching our every move.

"There's nothing to be done. What you did today was perfect." I don't like that, what will happen if I'm not around? I will need to make sure that there's always someone with her.

"When I found out that you were my mate, I was surprised. How could a witch be a demon's mate? But then when I met you, the feelings that overwhelmed me assured me that you are the only man that can ever make me happy—the only man that I can trust completely. And even though we are different, today you have shown me that demon or no demon, you care."

Since a very young age, I have lived in darkness and only seen pain. Now, out of the blue, I'm surrounded by light, caring, and peace.

I know that Raine will light my way, and even though I'm darkness, I know that her light will penetrate that blackness in my soul, and show me a fulfilment that I've never felt before until now.

Here in the Warriors MC, I found a family. Men that have their own horrors to live with but that stand together united against the world that has rejected us. It's a family that has given me protection and loyalty. Now that family is complete as I bring my mate—my woman—my very soul in to be a part of that family.

"My darkness is now a shade of grey because of you. The continuous void in my soul has been filled. You are my light. Without you, I'm blind to the reality of sensations that bring the meaning of life. Take from me the strength you need, the protection, and the promise of eternal loyalty."

Raine isn't just my mate, she is an explosion of sensations that are now stamped into my very DNA. She is my life.

A MIDNIGHT REVELATION

Warriors MC

ELLA 1

I hear the main door opening downstairs, which has me cringing in anticipation of what will be asked of me today. My father died in a shooting last year. Being the President for the Wicked Warriors MC had its dangers, so I should have been prepared. Instead, I hid behind the high walls of my university, lying to myself that everything would always be fine.

After my mother died, it was just the two of us. Because even though Dad had the MC, he always kept me far away from any and all club business, as he called it. After my mother's death, my father lost his way, drinking too much, and getting into things which he would never have done if my mother was still alive. I loved my father with all my heart, and I know that he loved me. The only thing that I held against him was marrying Trudie.

My dear stepmother is a real thorn in my side. The minute father died, she pulled me out of university. Even though I only had another five months to finish my degree, she insisted that there was no money to pay for my studies, and that I was needed at home. She takes every opportunity that she can to make sure that I get as much done during the day as humanly possible. Trudie was one of the patch whores in the club. I have no idea why dad would marry her after having my mother in his life.

Trudie has two daughters that are also club girls. They love throwing it in my face that I think I'm too good for them, just because I went to university. The truth is, I don't. I try to do everything that they ask of me and keep out of their way as much as possible. At twenty-one, I don't have many prospects because I wasn't able to finish my degree or able to look for work. I have no money and I have Trudie to thank for allowing me to live in my own home.

I make sure that I don't upset her; she has my life in her hands now, and there is nothing that I can do about it. I scrub at the angry tear streaking down my cheek. There's no use crying at the situation. The only thing that I can do is continue doing the best I can until I have found a way out of this situation.

"Ella?" I cringe when I hear Trudie's voice.

Oh mom, I wish you were still here. I often find myself internally pleading for my mother up in Heaven to save me from this life, but there really is no use thinking about things that I can't change.

Taking in a deep breath, I make my way towards the sitting room where I heard Trudie's voice come from.

"You're looking for me?" I can smell the alcohol the moment I enter the room. It's a constant stench that comes with Trudie, overwhelming me instantly.

"Yes, what took you so long?" she mutters as she lights a cigarette. Not waiting for my reply, she continues, "I told Zen that you would go and decorate the club for the Halloween party."

What? Zen has come to visit temporarily? He's from the Montana chapter, and I guess he's here to assess everyone and figure out which of the members would make the best President. After the shootout, the club lost my father known to everyone as throttle, also Rattler who was the VP, and one of the other MC members. It was only fitting for the Wicked Warriors mother chapter to send Zen in to assess the situation and place the appropriate members in my father's President and the newly opened VP spots.

I have only seen Zen a couple of times, and that's from a far. The only reason I know anything about him at all is because I overhear the things Jackie and Tammy say when they're home. I know that both have been fighting for his attention, but it seems like Zen is dead set on ignoring them. If I go by all the whining, they have been doing. All I can say is good for him; he hasn't fallen for their tricks yet.

"When? I still have a couple of things to finish." Trudie lifts her hand, pointing her index finger at me.

"You lazy, ungrateful bitch," she suddenly snaps. "What have you been doing since I left?" Looking at the clock on the wall behind her, I frown. It has only been about three hours since she left.

"I have done all the washing, cleaned Jackie and Tammy's rooms, taken the trash out, and cleaned the bathrooms." I see her scowl because I'm sure she wouldn't know how long each thing takes to do. She's not the domestic type.

"You are lazy and slow," she argues, then waves her hand, dismissing me. "You will just have to do everything with tomorrow's chores. Now go. Do as I say. Zen is waiting for you." I know that it's no use arguing because she won't listen to anything I say. I'll have to get up even earlier than I already do and go to bed even later.

Sighing, I make my way outside. The club is at the end of the road and I can make it there in five minutes, but today I decided to walk slower and enjoy the beauty around me. I haven't been to the club since my father died, and even before that, it wasn't often that I went there. My father wanted to keep me away from that life. I know most of the men at the club, and the men have always been respectful to me, something which I appreciate when I see how some of the women are treated.

"Hey, Princess, what brings you here?" Jack, one of the club's oldest members, asks me as I approach the building. He was one of my father's closest friends and I know that he misses him dearly.

"Hi, Jack. Trudie asked me to come down and help decorate for the Halloween party." I see a scowl darken his features as he inclines his head inside.

"Why can't the girls do it?" he asks, which has me shrugging as I take the step up towards the main door, hearing the music blaring inside. "I'll come with you, darling. I want to make sure that those young studs keep their hands to themselves." I stop and grin at his protectiveness.

"I couldn't ask for a better protector," I state as I wait for him to reach me before I once again make my way inside. The bar area looks different from when I was last here. It seems to be lighter and not the stale cigarette and alcohol smell that typically hits you when you entered the club.

"Well, well look who has come off her high horse." I tense when I hear Jackie's voice come from where she's sitting on one of the club member's lap.

Ignoring Jackie, I Look towards Jack. "Where can I find Zen?"

Jack inclines his head towards the far corner of the bar. Turning my head, I'm met with piercing dark eyes that hold my gaze as if he's looking deep into my very soul. The very air seems to have stilled around me. I have seen him riding past before, but I've never really seen him up close. I now understand why Jackie and Tammy are so obsessed with him. The man is absolutely drop dead hot. There is a calmness about him that screams danger. The very air seems stagnant as I see his eyes travel over my face and then my body in a slow, hypnotic way.

"Princess?" the guy with Jackie on his lap suddenly says, breaking the spell that Zen had me under. "You have turned into a real stunner." Rory has always been a sweet talker. I've known him since I was thirteen and he was seventeen. He has always been a ladies' man, and it's not surprising to see him with a woman on his lap, even if that woman is my stepsister.

"Hi, Rory," I say with a smile. I had forgotten how much I enjoyed these men's company.

"You are like a ray of sunshine that has just exploded into this place," he says with a wink that has me shaking my head in amusement.

"I see that you are still a sweet talker," I quip as I turn my gaze back towards Zen. The scowl on his face has me tensing. It doesn't look like he likes the help to be talking to his men. Making my way towards where he is sitting, I feel a knot tighten in my stomach. The closer I get, the more dangerous he seems. There is an animalistic quality to him that has the hairs on the back of my neck standing on end, my heart racing as if it is ready to jump out of my chest.

I've never had a reaction like this to anyone. I want to stand here and stare at him the whole day. I want to...

"Take a seat." His deep voice has me suddenly realizing that I'm standing here gawking at him. Hurrying towards the chair, I pull it out and sit down facing him. I can feel everyone's eyes on us as they wait for his next words.

He must have realized it because he's gaze suddenly snaps up and from behind me, I hear the rush of scraping chairs, and mutters from the three other men that were sitting at the table with Rory, making their way out.

"Have you got nothing to do?" his deep voice asks quietly. I glance back to see that he is talking to Jackie, her cheeks flush at being called out before me. Great, this is going to be something else she can hold against me.

"Umm, I thought you might need something," she says sweetly.

"Leave." His order sounds more like a growl. When his eyes return to me, there is absolute silence, and I have no doubt that everyone has gone far away from his wrath. This man commands respect. I've never seen it before, not even with my father.

"Trudie says you want to help decorate the club for Halloween?"

At his comment, I raise my eyebrows. She did, did she? Trudie is such a liar.

"Well, looks like that was a lie," he says, inclining his head towards the door. "You can go."

"No, it's okay. I'll help."

My outburst has him looking at me again for a tense minute before he replies. "Why haven't you been to the club since your father died?" His question surprises me.

"My father always kept me away from the club. Since his death, I haven't felt like I belonged here anymore." My voice breaks at the end of my statement. I miss having my father around—miss his burley voice waking me up in the morning.

"I hear that you were at university. Why didn't you finish your degree when you only had a couple of months left?" I tense at his question; I didn't expect him to ask me that.

"There was no money to pay for the rest of my studies." My reply has a scowl darkening his features, which has me start to stand as the knot in my stomach tightens another notch. His hand suddenly snaps down over mine, holding me in place.

"You will decorate the club. Anything you need, you ask me." His statement has me nodding. His hand was hot over my cold one.

"I will need money to go and buy the decorations. Also, if possible, can someone take me? It will be difficult to bring everything back in the bus."

His hand tightens on mine. "You don't have a car?" Again, I shake my head at his question. I loved the mini my father had bought me when I first went to university, but when he died, Trudie had to sell it to pay for my father's debt. It seems like I was living a lie. Everything I thought changed the day my father died. He is looking at me with a quizzical expression, which I can't read. The MC kutte he is wearing is open to reveal his big muscular body tensing beneath the t-shirt that is stretched tight over his wide chest. "I will take you."

"Wha… what?" I didn't expect him to volunteer to drive me around finding decorations for Halloween.

"I will take you, but you are riding with me, and seeing as Rory doesn't have much to do, he can drive the cage and wait to bring everything back." Riding with him? Usually, the men only take their Ol' ladies on the back of their bikes. I know that it's an honor to be riding with him, but he makes me nervous. Everything about him screams danger.

"I can go with Rory in the car. I have known him for years." My reply has his scowl darkening, which shows that he is someone that people don't usually contradict. "I'm sure you have a lot to do here," I try to appease.

He grunts at my feeble attempt as he finally lets go of my hand and stands. I expel a relieved breath, but it is short lived when he says, "Let's go."

ZEN 02

Her arms wind around my waist as I ride into town. I can feel her perky breasts pressing against my back, which has my gun digging into my lower back, but I don't care because I can feel her nearness. When I saw her walking into the club, it was like someone had just punched me hard in the stomach. The breath was knocked out of me with one single whiff of her unique essence.

When I saw the hurt in her eyes because of Jackie's comment, I wanted to jump over the table and rip Jackie's throat for hurting her. When Rory started to come onto her, I was on the verge of killing him. If he had continued, I would not have been able to stop myself.

I don't know what it is about Elle, but she is mine! Looking in the side mirror, I see the MC vehicle following us with Rory in the driver's side, looking disgruntled. When Logan, the MC President for the Montana chapter, told me that I was needed here, I was angry. To be taken away from everything I know and told that I had to find out who the fucking traitor was in this hell hole didn't sit well with me, that is until my heart started beating and everything around me lit up with color for the first time in my life.

No one here knows that I'm a demon. No one will ever know unless they hurt my mate. That is something I never thought I would be saying. I never thought I would be meeting my mate, the only one that makes me vulnerable, the only one that can now be responsible for my death.

As a demon, my life span normally would only be one hundred and fifty years, unless I found the one and only woman that is my mate. Now that I found her, the only way I will ever die is if my mate dies, and there is no way that I am going to let anyone near her whose intentions are to kill her. The colors of everything around me are overwhelming. I never thought that it could be so vivid. Also, this sense of worry for my mate is strange for me, as I have never cared for anyone or anything. Being a demon is being devoid of emotions, emotions that come crashing down once we find the one.

"Fuck!" I grunt under my breath as I pull up outside a store that caters to all the holidays with decorations. My cock is as hard as a fucking fire poker, from having my woman this close to me and not being able to take her. She knows nothing about what I am, or the fact that she's mine. I will need to break it to her, but I've never been one to be gentle. I've always been one to take what I want without regrets or worries.

"Umm, how much can I spend?" The rosy cheeks have me wanting to grab her and kiss her breathless. This woman could have anything she wants from me. If she only knew that the minute she walked into the club, she would be changing our lives forever; I think she would have run the other way.

"I'll come in with you, just get whatever you need." I point to an empty spot next to the bike for Rory to park. Turning towards the door, I place my hand low on Ella's back as I guide her inside. I can feel the slight tremor running through her body, knowing that she can feel the same magnetism between us that I can. Each minute we are together, when we touch, even if just like this, our bond will grow.

Fate has a strange sense of humor. She gave me a twenty-one-year-old girl, when I'm a thirty-five-year-old man with a mean streak that will frighten her into an early grave. Grunting at my own thoughts, I feel her tensing as she glances up at me. "If you would like to wait outside, I can get everything and then call you when it's time to pay?" Her hesitant tone has me berating myself for giving her the impression that I don't want to be with her, but I'm not the poetic type of guy.

"No!"

At my abrupt reply, I see her complexion pale. Fuck, that's all I need—my woman to fear me. Grabbing her arm, I turn her to face me, her eyes widening in surprise.

"Don't be scared of me," I growl in annoyance before I lower my head and take her lips in a possessive, blistering kiss. Her hands creep up my chest and have my cock twitching in excitement. Hearing someone clearing their throat, I raise my head, anger blooming over the fact that someone is interrupting us. A woman holding a little girl's hand is at the entrance waiting to come in. Her annoyed expression has me glaring at her, which has her blanching in fear.

"Oh, so sorry," Elle says quickly as she grabs my arm and pulls me out of the way. I'm so surprised at her actions that I let her have her way. When I look down, I see her cheeks are rosy with embarrassment, her long dark brown hair is lying around her shoulders, and her hazel brown eyes are like two huge saucers looking up at me. "What was that?" she whispers, making me want to kiss her all over again.

"You act as if you have never been kissed before," I state, and then the image of some asshole kissing her has my demon wanting to come out and behead some faceless fool.

"I'm not like that," she whispers as she looks around in embarrassment.

"Like what?" I ask.

"Like Jackie and Tammy," she says, raising her chin to look at me.

"Good, those two irritate me," I confess. Since the minute I walked into the club, they have been trying to get me to take them, which only annoys me and has me staying away from them as much as possible.

"They do?" she asks in surprise.

"Yes, why so surprised?" *Have they been saying differently?*

"It's just that most men like them. It's strange to hear a man say that they don't like them," she confesses, and I can detect a tone of resentment in her voice.

"It must have been difficult to come home to a new family when your father died." I know that her father used to go and visit her at university, and that he kept Trudie quiet until just before he died. I've heard from the men that the President loved his Ol' lady and daughter deeply, and that when he started messing around with Trudie after his wife died, that they were all surprised. I know that Trudie is always complaining about Elle, about what a spoiled brat she is, and how she does nothing because she thinks she's too good for everyone.

I don't know what it is, but I think there is more to that story than what meets the eye, and whatever it is, I will find out now that Elle is mine. "It wasn't easy, but we all made the best of it." Her tone is sad, but there is no resentment in her voice. I find that I don't like the sound of sadness in my woman's voice. *What the hell is happening to me?*

I have never worried about anyone's feelings, and always believed that feelings just got in the way, that I was so good at killing and seeing things objectively because I didn't have feelings obstructing my view of situations. That's why I was sent here to figure out who the traitor is that got the men killed. But now that Elle exploded into my life, all I can think about is what I can do to make her happy.

"Come, let's get what we need so I can get everyone to help decorate." My statement has her gasping as she looks up at me in surprise.

"You're going to get the men to help put these up?" I know why she has that reaction. When I first came to the club, the men were lazy fucks who just wanted to drink, shag, and fight. Since coming, I have started to set them straight, and the ones that didn't want to see reason, I showed it to them. After some violent convincing, they have all come around to my way of thinking, but I'm still not convinced about the devotion some of them have for the club.

"Yeah, if they want to continue their tradition then they need to help."

A smile suddenly appears on her beautiful face that makes me want to kiss her all over again.

"Can I please be there when you tell them?"

Her question has me shaking my head. "You don't believe that they will do it?" I ask, raising a brow.

"Oh, I'm sure they will do it, but I'm also sure that they will grumble the whole time." She shakes her head in amusement. "My mom, the girls, and I always used to decorate the club for the Toy Run Halloween party. I don't mind doing it."

"Well, it's time that they work for something they clearly enjoy," I state, not giving in to the fact that she is trying to get the guys out of the work. The club has been doing the Toy Run for all the homeless children, because it's a noble cause for many years, and the fuckers don't do many of those, I decided that we would continue with the tradition, but if they can't do the bare minimum to maintain the tradition, then I will cancel everything.

"So..." she starts, then bites her lip in uncertainty.

"So?" I ask.

"So, you only need me to buy the decorations?" I hear a sadness in her voice and realize that this tradition isn't only important to the men but clearly to her too, as she used to do this with her parents every year. Fuck, maybe I won't cancel it after all.

"No, I need you to organize the whole thing." To be fair, parties are not my forte, and I wouldn't know where to fucking begin. I know that I could just get Trudie to bang something together, but I have noticed from previous parties that we have had at the club that when she organizes the parties, all you get is booze and very little else. I'm a demon, and even though I can drink with the rest of them, I need my meat. Parties back home are all about food, and the men at our side we trust with our lives.

Here, it is clear to me that they don't trust each other, and that if they got half a chance, they would easily stab the guy next to him. For me, m MC is my family, and even though we don't always see eye to eye, we know that we can trust each other. I know that if anything happens to me, the others won't throw me under the bus. All the men back home are shifters, there are other demons, werewolves, bears and even a phoenix.

We are volatile, hard to handle, and downright mean when provoked. Most of us have scars that no one sees, but that shape our personalities. The one thing that we all have is values. We are devoted to our club, to each other, and when we find our mate, we're devoted to the woman that has given us back part of our soul.

"Is it just the men that are going to help?" Her hesitant question has me snapping out of my thoughts.

"No, the girls will help you too." My reply has something flash in her eyes, which I can't tell what it is, but she seems nervous when she nods, and then starts looking at the decorations the store has to offer. I grunt, as I follow her. This is the last thing I would ever think I would be doing, but I wouldn't trust my woman's life with any of the men.

Following her, I look down to see her sassy little ass swaying in her tight jeans, my cock hard and ready to make her fully mine. My hands are itching to grab her waist and pull her back against my hardness, to rub her body against mine. Fuck, this is going to be a long day!

ELLE 3

"You think you're all high and mighty now that Zen took you on the back of his bike, don't you?" Tammy says as she grabs my arm and pulls me back from where I was about to walk out of the bathroom. Her fingers dig into my arm, nails carving deep into my flesh. There will be bruises tomorrow for sure, but it won't be the first. Ever since coming back home, I have had to accept that my life has changed, and until I can find a way out, I will have to put up with this treatment.

"No, he just took me shopping for decorations." There's no way that I would tell her that he kissed me, not when I know that Jackie and Tammy have been trying to get it on with Zen. There is no way in hell that I would tell her that he took an interest in me. Unfortunately, it will be short-lived because sooner rather than later, Zen will be leaving to go back home, and I will still be living with Trudie and dancing to her tune.

"Listen here, you stupid bitch. You stay away from him. Do you hear me?" She tugs painfully at my arm before letting go and walking out of the bathroom. Sighing, I rubbed at my arm. *Oh, Daddy. I wish I could have finished my degree, maybe then I would have been able to get a job and stay far away from here.* Taking in a deep breath, I square my shoulders before walking out of the bathroom and back into the bar area where most of the club members are decorating. The others are outside, inflating the rubber ghosts and carving the pumpkins.

My heart is heavy in my chest as I look around. Three years ago, I was still doing this with my mother.

I jump in surprise when Zen suddenly grabs my arm at the elbow. "Who did this?" His voice has the hair on the back of my neck rising. There is a deadly quality to it that doesn't bode well for the person.

Pulling my arm out of his grip, I shake my head. "No one, it doesn't matter."

I can see the anger flashing in his eyes before he raises his head and looks around, his nostrils flare as if he is smelling something before he steps away from me and heads towards where three of the girls are standing and talking instead of untangling the make-believe webs that we had in storage.

"Don't you have anything to do?" Zen asks, which has all three of them looking around in surprise. "If you don't want to help, you can leave and don't come back." His harsh statement has them looking at him with shocked expressions.

"But we are part of the club," Jackie says in surprise.

"No. Being part of this MC requires devotion to the Wicked Warriors. It requires its members to do whatever it takes for the club. All I see you do is sponge off the men." I'm surprised at how harsh he can be.

"Are you going to let him talk to us like that?" Tammy asks, looking at the men that are inside. I look around too to see some shake their heads and turn their backs on them. Others continue looking, but don't interfere.

"You need to leave and don't come back," Zen says to Tammy as he starts to turn. He then stops to look at her with a furious expression. "Oh and tell your mother that if she wants to continue being part of this club, she better get her ass up here and start helping."

I'm so shocked at what just happened that I'm rudely staring. In a way, I feel sorry for Tammy because I know that this is her life.

Zen turns, heading outside. He glances at me on his way out and I know that Zen did this because of what Tammy did. Zen somehow knew that she was the one that confronted me. My heart tightens when I think that this was all because of protecting me. No one has ever gone to such lengths for me, no one has ever cared enough to fight for me.

I think back to our kiss at the store and how everything around me disappeared, how I have never felt like I feel when he touches me, kisses me. My father always kept me away from the club, saying that his daughter deserved to find herself a good man that took care of her like the princess she was. I met a couple of guys when at university and all of them were creeps. None made me feel like Zen makes me feel.

"Hey, Princess? What the fuck am I supposed to do with this?"

Looking at Rory, I smile when I see him holding up a skull with another two on the table in front of him.

"You found the graveyard."

My reply has his eyes widening as he lifts the skull at eye level. "Is that what I did?" he says sarcastically as he places the skull back down and looks in the trunk.

"That is supposed to go outside under the trees. You can arrange a little graveyard with the two tombstones, skulls and various bones in there." He shakes his head at my reply as he starts to place the skulls back in the trunk.

"You know, this is morbid. Why would anyone enjoy a party with graveyards and skeletons," he teases, knowing how much I love Halloween.

"If I remember correctly, weren't you the one that was found hugging a skull in a drunk stupor while lying in the so-called graveyard?" Jack quips from where he's unpacking the black sheets to cover the windows.

"I still swear that one of you orchestrated that whole scene," Rory says with a laugh as he points at me. "It was you, wasn't it?" I shake my head with a wide grin as he lifts the trunk on one side. "Could use some help here?" he mutters.

"They don't make men like they used to," Jack states as he drops the sheets and moves to help Rory with the trunk. "Come on, boy, let's go"

I smile, feeling for the first time the joy that I used to have every year when doing this with mom. Turning my head from them towards the door, I see Zen in the doorway. His eyes are intense as he watches me. The tattoo on his neck is dipping under the fabric of his T-shirt, making me want to pull it away to see what kind of art he has on his body.

The next few hours continue in pretty much the same fashion, and I'm surprised to see the men are enjoying what they are doing. Zen maintains aloofness from the others, only intervening when necessary.

Trudie came in a couple of minutes ago and immediately approached Zen. Her expression is one of remorse as she talks to him. I can't hear what they are saying from where I'm standing, but it's clear that she's spinning some lies that will have him take pity on her and bring Tammy back. A big tub with the pulp of the pumpkins that have been carved has just been brought in and now it's time to prepare it for pumpkin pies, and all the other treats that we usually make at this time of year.

"Would you like some help?" I look up to see Daisy, a quiet girl that has been with Rocky for a few months. He seems to really like her, but for some reason, he hasn't made her his Ol' lady yet.

"Yes, please," I reply with a smile. It's always nice to bake with company. "But you might change your mind once you see how much work there is."

"I..."

"You can't do that." Trudie's scream interrupts what Daisy was going to say. We both look towards where Zen is standing before Trudie with his arms crossed, a bored expression on his face.

"No," he says, and then he's turning and walking away, leaving Trudie with a stunned expression on her face. Since marrying my father, Trudie has taken it for granted that she can do what she wants, but what she doesn't realize is that my father has died, and she isn't the queen bee any longer.

Looking around, her eyes hardened. "What are you all looking at?" she screams.

"Oh boy, this isn't going to be pleasant," Daisy mutters as she turns back towards me, and then her eyes widen. "Oh, I'm so sorry. I didn't mean any disrespect, I know she's your stepmother and all."

I wave my hand in dismissal. "You're right," I whisper when I see Trudie approaching.

"This is all your fault," she says angrily as she points at me. "all you had to do was decorate this place for the party, but you couldn't even do that, and instead get everyone in trouble because of your incompetence." She points towards the door angrily.

"Leave, I will organize the rest and deal with you when I get home."

My heart tightens. I was enjoying doing this. For the first time since dad died, I felt at home, but I should have known that it was short lived. Nodding, I place the spoon on the table and start undoing the apron.

"No!"

Looking up and behind Trudie, I see Zen standing behind her with his hands on his hips. "Elle stays, and contrary to what you said, she has done a marvelous job and I doubt she can organize this party worse than the ones I've attended here." At his words, I see Trudie's face tense at being reprimanded.

"Fine, it's your funeral, don't say I didn't warn you," she snaps as she walks away and towards where the rooms are. I see Zen frown, and then he follows her.

"That was close," Daisy whispers. "I was starting to think of excuses to leave." Her words have me looking at her in surprise and then laugh as I never would have expected that from quiet Daisy.

"I think you're a dark horse," I quip as I elbow her playfully, only making her smile more. The rest of the day continues with no more hiccups, and soon the wonderful smells of baked goods are wafting about the club, which has the men coming in to steal little treats from the table when they think we're not looking. At the end of the night, I'm exhausted and can't keep from yawning every couple of minutes.

To be fair, I don't want this day to end. It has been so nice to be among everyone again, but most importantly, it's been thrilling to look up and have Zen's eyes always on me. I think that almost everyone has noticed, and I know that I will be paying for his attention once I get home. But for now, I'm enjoying it and letting tomorrow take care of itself.

"Come on, it's time for you to go to sleep." Looking up from the last tin of cookies that I have just finished decorating, I see Zen standing before the table with his hands low on his waist.

"I still have to…"

"No, you can leave the rest for tomorrow."

I sigh, knowing that there is no way that Trudie will let me be here tomorrow. My heart feels like someone is tearing a strip out of it when I think of not seeing Zen again, but now or later it's bound to happen, as he will leave here soon and go back to his club.

"Okay," I concede, as I'm finding it difficult to keep my eyes open. When I stand and start making my way towards the door, I'm stopped by his next words.

"Where do you think you are going?"

I frown. "To bed," I reply

"You're going the wrong way. Today you will be sleeping here." I feel like my heart has just skipped a beat at his statement, but then I see Trudie standing in the far corner glaring at us.

"Umm, I don't think so," I say as I fist my hands, preparing to leave, knowing that if I stayed, I would still be here tomorrow and be able to participate in the Halloween Party.

"I insist." His tone brooks no argument as he slides an arm around my waist and starts guiding me inside towards the rooms until we reach the last room at the end of the corridor. I know before he opens the door that this is his room, and he expects me to sleep with him.

"I'm sorry, but I'm not going to sleep with you."

He grunts at my words, but instead of letting me go, he closes the door behind us.

"You don't need to worry; I'm not going to attack you. We're just going to sleep."

I know that I'm being silly by believing him. After all, I should know better than to believe a man when he's alone with a woman in his room, but something about him makes me trust him, makes me want to take a chance even though I know that tomorrow when I must go back to my real life, things are going to be worse than ever.

"Okay." I don't know why, but I feel like I have just consented to much more than just spending the night in his room.

ZEN 4

My mood is foul today. After spending the night wide awake, watching my woman as she slept next to me in my bed, and not being able to touch her when everything inside me screamed at me for not coupling with her, I'm about a breath away from snapping.

We're about to head out to the orphanages; the toys have been attached to our Harleys, and everyone is getting ready to ride. Two other clubs have arrived to partake in this initiative and spirits are high. Looking towards where I know Elle is, I lift my hand, crooking my finger for her to come to me.

"You need something?" she asks when she comes to stand next to me.

"Yes, get on!"

My reply has her gasping and then she's looking from my bike to me. "You want me to go with you?" she asks in surprise.

"Yes, now hurry up so we can get this show on the road." I'm not one to smile often, but at the speed with which she gets on the Harley, I would say that she's excited to venture out on the bike. Her arms slide around my waist, and I feel like I have just come home with my woman's arms around me. We make our way out of the club grounds and towards the first orphanage. I was never one to care about these things, but when we are handing out toys and I see the joy on the children's faces, I feel something within me that chokes me up.

Fuck, why would anyone want feelings? It's clear that Elle loves doing this, and that putting a smile on these children's faces makes her happy. We spend a couple of hours with the kids, something which shows me that my childhood wasn't that much different from these kids that have no one to love them—no one to guide them in life. Instead, my mother didn't want anything to do with me once I was born. In true demon fashion, my father got tired of having me around when I was four, leaving me to care for myself.

When we get back to the club, I see that the fires are blazing, and the prospects have started the barbeque.

"Where are you going?" I snap, feeling uncomfortable with Elle around so many men I don't know.

"Daisy insists that we dress up for Halloween. She says that she has something for me to wear." She's looking unsure and from what I've gathered yesterday and today, things aren't what Trudie led us to believe. Therefore, I want Elle to have a great time without having to worry about her stepmother. Lifting my hand, I slide it around her neck, which has her sighing in surprise as her eyes widen.

"Make sure that once you have changed, you stay close to me. I don't trust half these fuckers." At my order, a huge smile breaks across her face, which has me lowering my head and kissing her lips with a passion that leaves both of us wanting so much more. If it wasn't for a club full of people, I would be taking my woman straight to my room and making sure that she knows who and what I am. I know that once Elle finds out what I am, it will be difficult for her to understand, as she has no idea that beings like me even exist. But the bond that we already have won't let her reject me, as she is the light to my very darkness, and she feels that as much as I do.

When I raise my head, her eyes are heavy with passion. "Go on," I encourage, looking after her as she disappears inside with Daisy. I make my way towards where the food is with my back to the wall, watching the men drinking and laughing. My eyes stop on one brother, and I tense. I know who the traitor is, but I'm waiting for him to slip up and reveal himself.

"You know, she's not like the others." I glance towards my left where Rory is standing with a bottle of beer in his hand.

"I know." From the interaction between him and Elle, I have come to realize that they see each other as friends, which is good, or I would have to kill the asshole.

"She deserves to be treated right." This time when I look at him, my eyes are hard, but I respect the fact that even though he is weary of me, he's standing up for Elle and making sure that I treat her right.

"I will treat her right," I promise.

"Good," he replies, stepping away from where he was standing and making his way towards a group of club girls that arrived with one of the other clubs. I see one of the women strolling towards me and I grunt in annoyance.

"What are you doing here all by yourself, darling? Would you like some company?" she asks as she places a hand on my chest. Pulling her hand off my chest, I let it drop to her side.

"No."

"Are you shy?" she asks with a simpering smile.

"Leave," I order, getting annoyed at her insistence.

"Fine," she mutters. "Your loss." I look to my left where loud voices have me tensing, but I see that there is nothing to worry about. The minute I feel the hand on my chest, I growl, my eyes snapping to the woman before me.

"Zen?" My name whispered from her lips has me stilling as if frozen in place as my eyes travel over her catsuit that molds every inch of her perfect body. Only her red lips are revealed. The top half of her face is covered by the same shiny fabric with two pert ears on the top.

"Fuck, you're sexy," I grunt, which has her smile as she looks down at herself and shrugs.

"Not my favorite Halloween character, but it will do," she says softly.

"What is your favorite Halloween character?" I ask with a raised brow as my arm slides around her waist and I pull her close against my body. I will never let Elle go again. I will deal with the lies that Trudie has concocted, I will find out where the money is that Elle's father left her, and why she was pulled out of university when it's clear that he always wanted her to finish. Trudie will pay for what she did, and so will the traitor.

"Demon." Elle's answer has me smiling.

"I'm your demon!" I reply. She doesn't know it yet, but she will soon. She raises her hand to my cheek, the eyes behind the mask soft.

"You might be a demon, but you are everything I have ever wanted." Then she is lifting on her tiptoes and kissing me with a sweetness that melts my heart.

THE END

LOVE UNLEASHED

DRACO 1

"I found that guy you were looking for." Glancing over at Celmund, I wait for him to continue.

Katrina has been all over the place since giving birth to Damon. I smile, thinking of our little boy. I don't know what kind of powers he will have once he grows up, but one thing I do know is that he has the power to wake everyone up. It has only been in the last week that he has finally slept right through the night. After ten months of not having a full night's sleep, Katrina deserves to be treated.

Valentine's Day is coming up, and even though I'm not the poetic chocolate type of guy, I decided to organize something for my woman that she will enjoy. I have arranged with Bion and Brielle to take Damon for the weekend, while I take Katrina away. She has no idea that I am organizing this, as I still need to convince her to leave our son, but I know that she will love what I have planned for her.

After finding my mate and bonding with her, my life has changed completely. The things that I found important for centuries have changed. The most important things in my life are my son, my club, my men and my woman's happiness. This is all about my woman's happiness. In the four years we've been together, I haven't treated my woman to anything special.

She has given me everything, and instead of the happy, peaceful life that she should have got, she has been through shootings, kidnappings, and turmoil. A couple of weeks ago, I heard her talking to Jasmine about how she would love to attend a concert where one of her favorite singers is performing. I have never been interested in attending a concert, and I will definitely not let Katrina be pushed around in a rush of people, but I will make sure that she listens to her favorite singer.

Since Damon's birth, we haven't had much time for ourselves, therefore, I decided to surprise her. Katrina says that I don't have a romantic bone in my body, I thought that I would show her that she's wrong, and I'm going to do it over Valentines. "Do you know that he's a shifter?" Celmund's words bring my thoughts to a standstill.

"What?"

"Yeah, the guy all the women go crazy about is a fucking shifter." I tense, I didn't expect that.

"Katrina's not crazy over him, she just likes hearing him sing." I know that Celmund is just trying to get a rise out of me, but I don't like to think of my woman looking at anyone else. "Tell me."

Celmund picks up a folder and hands it over to me. "He's Lupin, his pack are all a part of an MC. You might have heard of them; they are the Wolverine MC." Yes, King is their alpha. I had a run in with King a couple of years ago, but we sorted our differences out. One thing I realized about King is that he is just and a strong alpha to be reckoned with.

Opening the folder, I look at the photo Celmund has placed inside of the singer. I can feel myself tensing. The possessive side of me tells me to find something else to treat her with, but the mate in me knows that she's my woman, and nothing will ever change that. That side of me tells me to stop being an ass and organize this for her.

Lifting the photo, I look at the information on him. He clearly hasn't found his mate as it states here that he has had various women in his life in the last year. "I'm surprised King lets one of his pack leave for such a long time."

"From what I have picked up, this wolf is restless and doesn't stay with the pack for long." Celmund walks towards his computer, picking it up. He brings it over to me to show one of Blue Strada's concerts. I see the man sitting on a high stool playing the guitar, his voice isn't too bad.

"Organize the private concert," I order. We are fighting a fucking gang in Cape Town and trying to clear the streets for the Bratva because they have someone trying to undermine all their deals, but this is important. I need this weekend off with my woman so I can show her that *she* is important, and that she is the only thing on my mind.

"I will talk to his agent. From what I have read, he is a real shark, always ready to make a buck." Good, that is just what I wanted, a greedy son of a bitch that is willing to make an exception for money. "It looks like they were having problems a while back with a serial killer."

"One of them?" I can't see a Lupin being a serial killer, but there is a first time for everything.

"No, I don't think so. The cops looked into them but haven't found anything. That was about the time your singer took to the road again."

I doubt he's the serial killer, but if he is, I will be with my woman at all times. There is no problem that anyone will get close enough to hurt her.

"I'm not sure we can organize it for the fourteenth, you know its Valentine's Day, and lover boy has a concert for that day already booked," Celmund says as he places his laptop on the desk and turns to look at me again.

"You will just have to sweeten the deal enough until he accepts." I don't care if he does it before or after his concert, as long as he plays for my woman.

"When are you going to tell Katrina?" I shrug, still not sure if I'm going to tell her or keep it a surprise. One thing is certain, I am going to have to tell her that we are going away as I will need time to convince her to leave Damon. My woman has a mind of her own, and if I go about something the wrong way, I might not pull this surprise off. "I still can't believe you're doing this."

His murmured words have me raising my brows. "Why?"

"You are not exactly the show your feelings kind of guy, and who would have thought that Draco the all-powerful, would fall this low?" I should be offended at his joking comment, but I know that what he says is the truth. But when you love someone, you need to make exceptions. My phone starts to ring, interrupting our conversation. Looking down, I see that it's Tor. Tor is the Cape Town Chapter president, he doesn't usually phone unless there is a problem which immediately has me stiffening.

"Tor," I greet.

"Another of my fucking men have found their mates."

I grin at his angry grunt. He had an episode with Suraya, a woman with a gift for manipulating people's feelings. She thought that Tor needed a lesson in humility and decided to play with his feelings. Needless to say, Tor didn't find it funny and since then, he has been dead set against mates.

"They're falling like flies. One of these days it will be you." I know that will get him revved up.

"Fuck off. You know that's the last thing I need." Actually, it's the opposite. After finding my mate, I think that him finding himself a woman would be the best thing for him. Tor takes way too many chances, and I believe that if he found his mate he would calm down.

"So, who is it now?" just a couple of months ago, Dane, one of his men, found his mate. She was none other than a famous actress. Now apparently there is another that has found his mate.

"Dag," Tor grunts in annoyance. "Do you believe it?" Actually, I know about Dag. He has been in contact with me to try to get Katrina to find his mate, but it seems like every time they close in, she takes off again.

"You know, him finding his mate is a good thing." I see Celmund raise a brow which has me showing him the finger as I turn to make my way out of the computer room, hearing him chuckle behind me.

"No, it's not, them finding their mates is a fucking problem, they're already changing my club."

Now, it's me grinning as I think of all the changes that have happened here since the men found their women. Yes, finding our mates changes a club, but he will realize that it's for the better. "You are enjoying this, aren't you?" Tor has known me for centuries; therefore, he knows that him being displeased with the women changing his club will amuse me. Tor has a tendency for lavishness, and the raunchiest things imaginable. I can just imagine what the women are changing.

"Did they finally take down that Image of the naked woman behind your desk?" I hear him grunt and can just imagine his scowling face.

"They won't dare touch my Mona Lisa." He calls the image his Mona Lisa, but the painting is far from a Mona Lisa and more a Kama Sutra work of art. "Anyway, I'm calling because I think we might have a lead on the Keres fucker that is giving the orders to the gangs." I stiffen, we have been looking for the son of a bitch that has built a small group of surviving Keres, and guided them to continue their perverse plan in kidnapping and trafficking all women that could be Elemental mates.

We managed to destroy the Keres MC a few years ago and convert the Keres back to Elementals. Keres are Elementals that have lost their humanity and become evil—Elementals that have gone through their life without finding that one woman that will light their way and calm their souls. We thought that we had vanquished most of the ones that we couldn't convert, but a year ago, we found that there are still some out there fighting for evil.

"Who is he?" Fuck, I really don't need any more complications right now when I am planning on taking Katrina away.

"Have you heard of Aldor?" I frown. The name is familiar, but the Aldor I know died a century or so ago.

"No."

"That's the name I have. He seems to be the king pin in this trafficking ring down here." If there is a Keres that is purposely trying to undermine our future, I need to make sure that I am involved. Fuck, I was trying to keep club business out of our weekend away, but it seems like I will have to make an exception. Good thing that the concert is in Cape Town.

"I'm coming down next week, you can show me what you have," I state as I walk outside to see Bjarni and Wulf riding up.

"Fine, I'm thinking of throwing a party," he snickers as he continues, "the women will love it." I shake my head at his sneakiness. Tor's parties are wild, and I imagine the mated women at the club won't like them.

"Katrina is coming with me." I warn, knowing that Tor has a soft spot for Katrina and won't do anything to upset her.

"Fuck, you're a real buzz kill, you know that? I don't know why I still call you?" With those words, he disconnects, leaving me shaking my head at his despondent tone.

"What's up?" Wulf asks as he approaches.

"Tor is having women problems." At my statement, Wulf raises a brow. Everyone knows that Tor is a tease, a real ladies' man. The only problem he ever had before meeting Suraya was the women flocking around him. "His men's mates don't seem to like the way he has decorated the club." Bjarni and Wulf grin at my words, knowing as well as me, how much Tor likes to shock.

"Talking about Tor, I'm going to Cape Town next weekend."

Wulf scowls. I haven't mentioned this to him before. Wulf is my right hand, best friend, and VP, so he usually knows all my moves.

"Tor thinks that they have found the head of the trafficking ring."

"Do we know the fucker?" Bjarni asks.

"His name is Aldor."

Both of them frown, which tells me that they both are coming up blank. Usually if it's an elemental elder, we will know the name.

"Aldor died, didn't he?" Wulf mumbles with a thoughtful expression.

"That's what I was told," I reply as I turn to make my way towards my bike. Whoever this Aldor is, we will soon find out, and when we do, he will be dead too.

KATRINA 2

I know that Draco meant well, but I don't know if I'm liking this idea. The thought of not seeing Damon for a whole weekend has me nervous. It's not because I left him with Brielle and Bion. I know they will take care of him like no one else would. But what if he misses me? Draco places his hand over my knee and squeezes gently.

We are on our way to Cape Town, and to be honest, it's not the most brilliant plan of Draco's. Why the hell would he think that going to the Cape Town chapter would be exciting for me? I have always told him how happy I am to go back home. Men never really listen to what we say.

"Relax, you're supposed to enjoy this weekend." Draco's words are barely heard over the sound of the wind as his

Harley speeds towards Cape Town. Draco's thumb strokes gently over my leg, trying to distract me.

Tightening my arms around his waist, I lay my head against his back. The heat from his body warming my front. In one way, I have missed this alone time with Draco. Since having Damon, we have not had any alone time. I know that I've been complaining about it, but now that he is giving it to me, I'm not sure I want it—not when Damon isn't with us.

"I'm worried about Damon," I whisper, but I know that Draco will hear me.

"Damon will be fine. Now stop worrying. If anything happens, Bion will contact me."

I grunt in irritation. "This better be good," I mutter as I stroke my fingers up and down his torso

"You are playing with fire."

I smile at his tone, my hand moving lower until it's cupping an impressive bulge. "You should know by now that I love your fire."

Draco's hand snaps over my wandering fingers, holding them still over his crotch.

"You're going to pay for teasing me, you minx." His growl has me smiling. Maybe this could be interesting after all.

Bjarni and Burkhart are accompanying us for the weekend. None of the Elementals are allowed to ride alone, no matter who they are. Luckily, they are riding behind us, and can't see my naughtiness. Draco told me that I didn't need to bring anything as he organized everything for this weekend. I hope he organized some nice lingerie, because I feel like dressing up and seducing my man.

When I first met Draco, I was blown away by his presence, by the very animalistic energy around him. I have a gift—a gift of finding anything or anyone I want. But when I found Draco, the man that I knew I was supposed to be with, I thought my instincts were wrong. Draco has been a dream come true. Yes, it hasn't been easy with all the turmoil that has involved the club, but Draco is a rock. If I have a problem, a worry, or anything that fears me, Draco will be there to keep me grounded.

Draco isn't just there for me, but for his whole club. His men depend on him, trust him, and will lay down their lives for him, but that responsibility doesn't come easily. Draco has more responsibilities than anyone else I have ever seen. That also complicates our time together, as we are always trying to find time to be alone. But one thing I can say about Draco is that he makes me feel, at all times, like the most important person in his life. He would drop everything if I had to ask him to.

I know that Draco is feared by most men, and with good reason as I don't think there is a man more powerful than him, but what humbles me and makes me love him even more, is the fact that even though he is the most powerful, he isn't a showoff.

The bike starts to slow. Looking around Draco, I see that we are pulling up at a gas station. Great, maybe we can get some snacks and have a nice cup of coffee. When I was pregnant, I was explicitly told to lay off the caffeine; I have been making up for it ever since. Stopping the bike, Draco helps me off.

I'm about to step around him to make my way inside, when his hand snaps around my upper arm. "Where do you think you are going?" Glancing up, I open my mouth to tell him that I was headed inside, when he surprises me by covering his lips over mine. Every thought of caffeine disappears, and I'm filled with the taste of Draco. His arm encircles my waist, pulling me closer to his body. I can feel his hardness heating up my body. I know we are kissing in public like two teenagers or two horny goats, but I don't care as the only thing that matters is my man's lips over mine and the way he always makes me feel.

I don't know how long he kisses me for, it could be seconds or hours because once Draco touches me, everything around me disappears, and the only thing that matters is the man that is holding me. "Hurry up," his whispered words against my lips have me snapping back to reality.

"I will take as long as I need," I murmur before taking a step back and turning.

I hear him grunt in humor. "I guess I'll be coming in there and carrying you out." His words have me tensing as I stop to look over my shoulder at him, I see his eyebrow rise at my surprise.

"You wouldn't?" I don't know why I ask, because I know that he would. Draco doesn't make idle threats; what he says, he always means. He doesn't respond, just looks at me with that penetrating blue gaze of his, which has me sighing. Guess I better hurry up, I look over to where Gabriella and Saskia are approaching the door, there pace hurried. I guess they were given the same orders. Gabriella is Bjarni's mate and mother to their twins, a beautiful boy and girl, and Saskia is Burkhart's mate.

We are all wearing our Kutte's because the men will not let us travel on the bikes without them, especially in situations like these. "I really need to pee, will one of you please get me a coffee?"

"Sure," Saskia replies as she heads towards the coffee machine

"Guess you got the same hurry up speech," Gabriela quips as she beats me into the lady's room.

"Yeah, but I'm not leaving here without having coffee." I know I sound like an addict, but I'm cold. Besides, I also want to make a call to Brielle to make sure that Damon is okay. "Can I use your phone?" Draco took my phone away, saying that this weekend was to relax and not worry about anything but enjoying myself. The only problem is that I am worried about Damon and will only relax once I know everything is okay.

Gabriela laughs at my request as she pulls her phone out of her back jeans pocket. "Took your phone, did he?"

I nod at her question as I place the call to Brielle.

"Gabriella, everything okay?" Brielle answers.

"It's me, I just wanted to know how Damon is?"

When she hears my voice, she laughs. "Sneaky," she murmurs, I can hear the smile in her voice. "He's fine. I just put him down for his nap." Her words have me relaxing as I enter a stall.

"Thank you, please don't tell Bion, I phoned, or he might tell Draco." I hate asking her this, but Draco is trying to make this a time just for us without our son, because of my complaints of never having time alone with him. I don't want him to know that I'm sneaking calls home.

Brielle laughs, "Your secret is safe with me." I disconnect the call before relieving myself. We have been riding for nearly an hour and a half, usually the men take breaks, but because of the war between the Elementals and the Cape Town gang The Desperados, they are taking more care. Stepping out of the ladies' room, I find myself walking straight into Draco's chest.

Looking up, I frown. "What, I had to pee?"

He raises one of his brows and I know that he suspects I made that call.

"There is someone following us."

Draco's words have me tensing. "Great," I mutter when he places his arm around my waist. "I thought we were going to have some nice alone time together, but instead, we are going to the Cape Town club that always has my hackles rising, and now we have trouble following us." I know this isn't Draco's fault, but for once I wish it would just be normal instead of the constant fighting. I can sense Draco's anger, but I know that he's not angry at me but at the situation.

"Fine, I'll get rid of the threat." I know by his tone that whoever has had the bad idea to follow us is in for a bad time. One person you don't want to anger is my man, because he will be your worst nightmare. Stopping, I turn, placing my hands on his chest to look up into his eyes.

"Let's just get to the club and away from whatever is following us. I just want to be with you with nothing to worry about. Can we do that?" His body is pulsing with pent up anger, I know that he wanted to make this weekend perfect for me, but he can't change what he is, or the fact that trouble follows us.

He reluctantly nods.

I lift on my tiptoes and kiss his lips before pulling back. "I love you." My words have his muscles relaxing slightly, and the hardness of his jaw soothing.

"You're a minx, and I know what you're doing," his deep voice whispers against my lips as he kisses me gently.

"Is it working?" I know that I can calm Draco, but the fact that I'm with him and there might be danger, will have him on edge. Nothing will calm that anger in him, not until I'm safe.

"You know that your touch has a special effect on me."

I smile at his statement. "Perv," I tease. "I was talking about calming you, as you know, and not about the erectness of your impressive manhood." The flash of those dimples as he grins at my teasing has me calming, knowing that he's less liable to kill whoever is after us now that he's calmer.

DRACO 3

"I was expecting you later," Tor calls from the door to the club as we take off our helmets. Placing my arm around Katrina's shoulders, I guide her towards the club and Tor.

"Thought we would surprise you," I say, which has him grinning, but by the way he's holding himself, I'd say that he's hiding something. "We have a tail. Get some men to go welcome him here for a talk, would you?"

I see Tor's eyes harden with anger as he nods. "Tal, Einar" he bellows as he glances over his shoulder. A minute later the two men are stepping around him.

"There's a fucker that needs a lesson in manners, bring him here." Einar nods his greeting; Tal grins and holds out his hand, which I take in greeting.

"Who is it?" Einar asks with a raised brow.

"In a dark blue Ford Mondeo. He has been following us since we left home," Burkhart states as he joins us, hand in hand with Saskia.

"Do you have any idea who he is?" Tor asks as he inclines his head for us to follow him inside.

"Human," I mutter, knowing that I didn't feel any other vibration that could pertain to an Elemental or Keres. Tor nods as he takes a seat at one of the tables in the Elementals CT MC chapter bar. He indicates with his hand for Camille, one of their jezebels, to bring us drinks.

"Well, let's drink and forget the tail for now. When such beauty is present, there's no place for depressing talk."

I grunt at Tor's sweet talk. He's not as bad as he used to be, but he is still a ladies' man, and the women love him. Tor can talk the birds out of the trees when he wants to.

"And you bring us Gabriela," he looks behind me as Bjarni and Gabriela approach. "Sweetheart, you can't leave without making those brownies of yours."

"She's on holiday," Bjarni states as he pulls out a chair and takes a seat, pulling his woman onto his lap.

"Don't be selfish. I know you want to keep her talent all to yourself," Tor says with an exaggerated scowl, which has the women laughing.

"I hear two of your men are now mated, I'm sure one of them will know how to bake."

Tor grunts, "If they do, they haven't shown us their talents yet," he grumbles, frowning.

"What other talents does Dane's woman have?" I like to keep track of what each of the mates can do within the Elementals. We never know when it could become useful.

"Don't let Eirik hear you. He is fascinated with her gift. When they were attacked a while ago, she saved his life, and since then, he has become her champion," Tor reveals as he sits forward, taking the beer that Camille has just placed on the table. "She can stop people in their tracks, they are completely frozen in place. You can punch them, and they won't know what happened."

"Oh, that's so cool. Imagine if she can freeze Draco in his tracks, and I can do anything I want to him," Katrina teases with a naughty smile at me. The minx knows just how to get my mind going. She knows that comment will get my imagination flaring. My body responds to her teasing, my cock straining against the zipper of my jeans.

"Careful what you wish for as the tables might be reversed." She knows that I can hold her down without even touching her, having my way with her when she is aware of everything but unable to do anything about it. I see her cheeks darken in excitement, I know that she's thinking back to other times.

"Get a room," Tor quips, grinning at us.

Dane and his mate walk into the bar. Looking at her, anyone can tell that she's completely in love with her mate, her very energy radiates it. Celmund acquired all the information he could about her, which at first puzzled me how a well-known actress would give everything up for her mate. Even though I know that Elementals bonds with their mates is strong, but I thought that she would have thrown more of a fight than she did.

"Welcome to the best Elementals chapter," Dane says with a grin as he approaches.

"In your dreams," Burkhart replies.

"Nah, my dreams are way too busy these days to dream of you."

Burkhart shows Dane the finger before he chuckles in amusement.

"I'm glad you're not dreaming about my man, or I would have something to say about that," Saskia teases. "Hi, I'm Saskia, so sorry you have to put up with this tease."

"Nice to meet you." She seems timid, which is strange for an actress.

"Freya, this is Draco," Dane says as he inclines his head towards me. "Draco is the Elementals National President."

I see her analyze me, which is good, it tells me that she is cautious. Sensing her energy, I feel its calmness telling me that she is at peace being among us.

"I have heard a lot about you," she murmurs.

Her words have me raising a brow towards Dane. He shrugs as he slips his arm around Freya's waist.

"You guys have arrived just in time for the party. Tomorrow we are bringing the house down," Tor says as he swings on his chair, the fucker knows I hate his lavish fucking parties.

"We won't be at the party, we have plans."

My comment has Tor dropping the chair on all fours. Katrina glances at me, a surprised look is on her face. I would rather she not know what is happening, but fuck me, if Tor thinks that we are going to attend one of his debaucheries. I have found that through the years, that he can be highly creative when it comes to shocking others with the depravity that he can come up with in his parties.

"Are you guys also not attending?" he asks, looking at Burkhart and Bjarni.

"I would rather not have to fight to keep all the drunk women off my man," Gabriela says as she rubs the back of her head against Bjarni's chest. Bjarni grins at Tor as he waggles his eyebrows.

"What about you?" Burkhart shrugs and inclines his head towards me.

"Sorry, man, I have to ride with Draco. You know the rules, no one rides alone." Burkhart knows about the concert and he asked if he could bring Saskia. Apparently, she also loves this singer. I would rather it be just Katrina and me, but I can't ignore my own rules, so I conceded. They won't be sitting with us, I want this to be all about Katrina and me. My woman wanted romance; I will give her romance.

"You guys have no idea what you are missing," Tor says with a shrug.

"Oh, yes we do," Katrina mumbles before she continues. "You know, Tor, I can't wait for you to find your mate. Please tell Draco the moment you meet her, because I want to be close to watch."

I shake my head, grinning at my woman's cheekiness.

"So, do I," Gabriela says with a laugh. "I want to see the poor woman's face the first time she sees Tor's parties or his room."

Tor scowls at their teasing, but I know that he finds it amusing that he is able to shock those around him. "What's wrong with my room?" he asks innocently, something that we all know he isn't.

"What isn't wrong with it?" Saskia sighs as she shakes her head exaggeratedly. "Your mate won't know if she has just entered Arabian Nights or if she should run."

"She will love it," he says, grinning at the women.

I laugh.

"If she's studying to become a nun or someone in that cloister, she would definitely love your room."

Katrina's comment has him looking worried all of a sudden, causing me to chuckle.

"Would serve you right."

He is about to answer me when Tal and Einar walk in. A man in his late forties walks in before them, looking scared shitless.

"This the fucker that was following you?"

At Einar's question, I nod as I go stand behind Katrina. If anything happens, I want to be close to her. Looking at Bjarni, I incline my head towards the man. Bjarni, as the Enforcer for the Elementals mother chapter, will be the one to get answers out of this asshole.

"I don't want any trouble," he says before we can ask him anything.

"Then why were you following us?" Bjarni asks as he goes to stand next to the man. Tal and Einar continue standing behind him, which by the way he keeps glancing back, has him intimidated.

"I want to be part of your MC; just thought I would wait for the right moment to approach you."

Tor starts to chuckle

"Sorry, we don't need accountants," Dane quips from where he is standing with his woman.

"Lift your arms," Bjarni orders.

With the way the man's back straightens and takes a step back, it's clear that he's hiding something. "Why?"

"Up," Bjarni snaps, but as he takes a step towards the man to frisk him, the man turns as if he's about to run, forgetting that Tal and Einar are still standing behind him.

"Going somewhere?" Einar asks in a conversational voice.

"You can't do this, I have rights," he cries out in desperation.

"You should have thought of those rights before deciding to follow us," Bjarni grunts, pulling the man's wallet out of his pocket. Opening it, he frowns, then he turns and brings it to me. "Looks like we have become famous." Taking the wallet, I look down to see a card. Our tail is a journalist—a journalist that is trying to sniff out information about us.

"Why were you following us? Think carefully before you answer, as it might be your last," I say only to feel Katrina's hand on mine. I would rather not question this asshole while the women are present, but there is nothing to be done about it now.

He turns, I can smell the fear radiating from him. Whatever this asshole might be hiding, he isn't leaving here without me knowing why he was after us. "I...I am writing about...about your MC," he stutters.

"Really? And who said you could write about us?" Bjarni asks with a scowl, none of us like anyone to delve too deeply into our lives for obvious reasons.

"No one has ever been...been able to get close enough to write about your MC. I want the story. I will write the truth about who the Elementals are."

"Look here, asshole, if..." I place my hand on Bjarni's shoulder which has him glancing at me and quieting.

Taking a step towards the man. I can see the tremor that races through his body.

"No." I don't care what he wants. If he persists, we will stop him, but there will be no story about us. His eyes widen at my statement.

"You cannot stop me."

I raise my brows at his statement and see him swallow in nervousness as I hear Tor grunt in amusement.

"Can you believe this asshole?" Tor stands and stops next to me. "He actually thinks that we are going to let him snoop into our lives."

"Look, if you will just talk to me, there will be no need for me to snoop."

I approach him, not in a hurry because no matter what, he will not write about us. Placing my hand around his neck, I lift him off the floor holding him against the wall.

He gasps, his feet kicking.

"Listen and listen carefully. You are going to desist, or you won't be breathing." I tighten my grip, his breathing becoming labored.

"You…you can't," he says breathlessly, "do this."

"Last warning, stop this now or we will stop you." With those words I let go of his neck, letting him drop to the ground.

He places his hand over his neck, breathing raggedly, his eyes tearing. I turn, walking back towards my woman. It's time I start giving my woman a great weekend like I promised her. Placing my hand on her upper arm, I pull her to her feet. "Let's go." I see her surprise, but she nods.

KATRINA 4

"That was hot." Draco looks at me with a surprised look, but it's true. His calmness and animalistic force, and how he holds himself when he wants something is incomparable.

"Since when do you like force?" he asks as we walk into the room.

As I turn to answer him, I'm suddenly off the floor. He picks me up, his hands under my ass as he takes my lips in an overpowering kiss that has me forgetting everything but his touch.

When Draco touches me, there is nothing else that matters, he has always been my ambrosia. His touch on my skin is like the stroking of my very soul. "I don't like force unless you use it on me," I whisper when he finally breaks the kiss. I know the minute I tease him, that he will take me up on it, but I know that anything that Draco could do to me would never bring me pain as he is incapable of hurting me. His dimples flash as he grins at my challenge. His hand fists in my long auburn tresses, pulling it back to expose my neck for his pleasure.

"Mmm, I think this weekend has just got a lot better," I murmur as his lips kiss down my neck; my legs still circling his waist as he holds me up with his other arm. My nails digging into his muscular arms, feeling his muscles contracting under my fingers.

"You have no idea," he whispers as he carries me towards the bed, dropping me onto the mattress. Laughing, I look up at him as he stands at the edge of the mattress, his magnetic blue eyes intensely looking down at me. Lifting his hands, he pulls his kutte off, placing it over the back of the chair near the bottom of the bed. His T-shirt is next to be pulled over his head, displaying his tattoos and twinkling gold hoops that hang from his pierced nipples.

I sit up, my eyes fixed on his body as I pull my shirt off. My hands move to the clip at the back of my lacy white bra when my arms are suddenly suspended above my head by an invisible force. My eyes clash with his to see the passion burning in his eyes. From previous experience I know that no matter what I do, I won't be able to get away from this invisible grip, unless he wants me to.

I have been asked before if being mated to a man like Draco worries me—a man with unrestrained power like he has, but my answer is always the same. Draco is the most controlled man I know. He can make me gasp with pleasure with his eyes alone. I don't fear Draco's power, because my power over him is just as strong as his over mine. He loves me with all his being. He shows it to me every single day, and I love him with everything in me.

"Unfair," I whisper as he places his naked knee on the bed, having just taken off his jeans. His body is a picture of perfection—of drooling sexiness.

"Do you remember teasing me while we were riding?" his low voice vibrates across my skin, caressing everywhere it touches. I see his palms are flat on the bed next to my hips, his torso lowering until his lips are over my lacy bra.

"Mmm hmm," his warm breath on my covered breast has my senses tingling. I feel his teeth scraping over my nipple before they clamp down. He pulls at my bra until I hear a tearing sound, which has me groaning when the cool air touches my sensitive nipple. His lips clamp down and he bites just hard enough to make me pay attention. His knee slips between my legs as his strong hands take hold of my hips.

"Let go of my hands," I murmur, wanting to touch him, but the invisible handcuffs that he is using, wielded by energy, hold me in place.

"No." His growled reply is followed by a nip that has me gasping for breath as his hand on my waist moves towards my breast while he continues to nibble and lick at my pebbled nipple. His finger and thumb start caressing my other breast, moving towards my nipple as he rotates it between his fingers. An overwhelming sensation of heat racing through my body, pooling between my legs with anxious anticipation, his knee rubbing against my most sensitive womanhood.

My jeans are an obstacle that I would gladly tear off. "Draco, stop teasing," I sigh, as he lifts his head to smile at me, knowing just what torture he is wrecking on my senses.

"Fair is fair, you teased me, now it's my turn."

I groan knowing that he is far from done, but suddenly I feel the pressure on my wrists loosening, which has me lowering my arms around his neck as he leans up to kiss me. His warm lips press against mine, his tongue dancing with my own, building a fire deep within me. Draco kisses every thought right out of my mind, building the expected outcome that leaves me wanting more.

Drawing my fingers through his hair, I grab at it, pulling it with passion. His grunt of pleasure is a spark firing my desire higher, making me want this man in a way that consumes my mind with his animalistic prowess. His hand slides down my torso to the button on my jeans. When he lifts his head, he sits back to fist the hem of my jeans, pulling it down my legs. I can feel my panties sliding down too.

"You are beautiful."

I smile. Draco is always telling me how beautiful he finds me. No matter how many times I hear him tell me, I don't get tired of hearing the words. It tells me that my man finds me sexy—that I please him in every sense, and it's not just our bond or mating that has him enamored with me.

His hands start stroking over my legs, his eyes holding mine as he continues touching me—loving me. When it comes to how this man feels for me, I can see it in the way he treats me, in the way he looks at me, and in the way he makes me feel. I feel like the luckiest woman alive for having Draco in my life, for having found my soulmate.

Draco is a great partner, friend, and lover, but he is also the best father for our child that I could ever have wished for. Suddenly he is grabbing my legs, with a tug he pulls me closer to him.

Before I know it, he has my foot in his hand. Lifting my leg, he kisses my calf, making his way slowly up my leg. My eyes close as I enjoy his touch—his kisses. "I can kiss and worship your body for an eternity." His voice is laced with restrained passion, my heart speeding its rhythm as I feel his kisses nearing my very core.

"Draco." I'm not sure if I whisper or shout his name. When his lips finally touch my glistening womanhood, my leg is now bent over his shoulder. His hand moves under my ass so he can raise my lower body to meet his ardent ministrations. Gasping, my hands pull his head closer, his tongue driving me closer to my release.

He plays my senses like a well-tuned guitar. "Draco, please," I gasp as he continues to torture me with his tongue.

"What do you want?" His deep voice is like molten lava flowing through my veins.

"You."

I feel him draw back, my leg dropping onto the bed. Opening my eyes, I smile as Draco places both his hands under my ass, lifting me up just enough for him to slide his pulsing cock deep into my depths. We both sigh in pleasure when he is buried deep inside of me. "Every time feels like the first time," I mumble as he pulls out slowly, making me groan before he plunges back in. "Ohhh." This man has my body tingling, every nerve ending fighting to explode with passion.

Draco makes love to me like a man drowning. Every thrust is a breath of passion, driving us both to the brink of release. "Yes, yes!" I scream when my orgasm takes me over the edge, the twinkling lights behind my closed eyes like a rain of falling stars.

"Kat," Draco grunts just as I feel him fill me with his essence, my body contracting around his, taking everything that he is offering. Opening my eyes, I see Draco's head thrown back, his muscles glistening and straining as he finds his release.

"You killed me." My words have him opening his eyes to look at me, his expression relaxing as his eyes soften. The fingers holding my hips relax as he starts stroking my skin gently where his hands are.

"You seem alive to me." He smiles when I groan as he pulls out. Standing, he walks around the bed to prop up the pillows before sitting down, leaning back against the headboard.

"Barely."

His hands move under my shoulders, pulling me up towards him until my head is on his shoulder. I love his strength, the way he makes it seem so easy. Draco makes me feel safe, no matter what is going on around us, he always makes me feel like nothing could hurt me.

"We have had a long day, just relax, and tomorrow I have a surprise for you." His statement has me lifting my head to look at him. He doesn't open his eyes, but he smiles, knowing that telling me he has a surprise for me just makes me curious to know what it is. "Don't ask because I'm not telling you," he says just as I open my mouth to ask him.

Huffing playfully, I slap his chest before laying down again. I smile. It's sweet of him trying to surprise me—going out of his way to make me feel special.

Lying here with Draco, but not hearing our little boy in his cot, makes me miss him. "I miss Damon," I whisper, not wanting to burst this bubble of contentment that we are both in. I know that Draco heard me, and for a minute I think that he's not going to answer, but then he lifts his hand and I feel a gust of wind just as I see his jeans lift from the floor, he is bending air to bring his jeans towards him instead of lifting me from his chest and getting up.

When the jeans are on the bed next to us, he pulls his phone out of the pocket. No matter how many times I see him bending the elements, it never grows old. "Hey, how's my son doing?" I smile at his words, lifting my head to meet his gaze.

"He's not going to want to go back home, Brielle is spoiling him rotten," Bion says, only now do I realize that Draco has placed the phone on speaker.

"Is he still awake?" Draco asks.

"No, he's been asleep for about half an hour now." Bion replies and I can hear the smile on his voice. Bion and Brielle still don't have children, so they usually babysit for everyone else. I know that Brielle would like nothing more than to have Bion's baby, but with the Elementals, pregnancy happens when it has to happen, and there's nothing anyone can do that will change that. There is no birth control when it comes to them; human birth control doesn't work.

Brielle was becoming despondent a couple of months back about not having children yet, but then one day, Orion told Brielle that her son was coming. We have all learned to believe in Orion's predictions as everything he has said has materialized. Orion is Wulf and Jasmine's son, and the first-born Elemental in the Nature Valley MC. Speaking of Orion, I forgot to tell Draco what Orion mentioned to me yesterday, this will be something that will please this man of mine.

"Good night, Brother," Draco calls before disconnecting the call. "Better now?" he asks as he leans over the edge of the bed to place his jeans and phone on the ground.

"Thank you. I was just worried that Damon would have started a fire or something without us there."

I see him frown at my cryptic reply. "He doesn't even walk yet, I'm sure he won't be getting into much trouble for a while," he quips as he leans down to kiss my forehead, missing my hint.

"Well, I don't know. From what I hear, bending fire can start early."

I feel Draco's abs tensing under my hand, his eyes open, and he looks at me.

"Damon is a fire bender?" he asks, a smile starting to lift his lips. "How do you know?"

"Orion told me."

He nods, the smile turning into a grin. "Fire bender is good. I will teach him how to control his power." I can hear the happiness in Draco's voice. "He will be burning everything around him until he learns."

"He better not, or I will be blaming his father."

Draco chuckles, slapping my naked ass playfully. "Have I told you lately how much I love you?"

His words have me smiling as I once again lower my head to his chest, listening to his heart beating under my ear. I feel his lips kissing the top of my head as I close my eyes. Yes, Draco loves me, but I love him just as fearlessly.

DRACO 5

"Just a hint?"

Katrina has been trying to figure out what her surprise is ever since I woke her up this morning, but that was my plan. I know that she loves surprises and gets excited like a child waiting at Christmas for its presents. I know that she's going to love the concert and hopefully the dinner and everything else I have arranged for her.

"You know I'm not going to tell you, why do you insist?" I ask with a smile as I pull her closer to kiss the top of her head.

"I'm trying to wear you out."

I grin, shaking my head as I guide her towards the bar where I can already hear men talking. I know that the Cape Town Chapter is the last place I should have brought Katrina if I wanted romance, but first comes her safety, hers and the other two women that my men brought who are accompanying me. I will make this Valentines one she will never forget. She has been so wrapped up with our boy from the moment he was born that she has tired herself out, even though I have tried to help her as much as possible.

Katrina was scared of being a mother when she found out that she was pregnant. I knew from the moment I met my woman that she would be my mate, and that included being the perfect mother. Katrina gives her all to anything she does and to anyone she loves. Katrina has given herself to me fully and completely, the same as me. I will always place my family before anything or anyone else. My woman and my child are my life, my brothers and their women are my family.

I would die for anyone in my club, my men and I have been together for centuries. We know everything about each other. There is an underlying vein of norms and values instilled in all of us that talk to the unbreakable bond that we all have with each other. When each one of us found our mates, it was a weight off our shoulders because we were all secretly apprehensive about what would happen if one of us changed into a Keres.

I held on for dear life, fighting my inner self to maintain an Elemental, not letting my baser evil side take over my mind, my body, and my very soul. I tried to protect all my brothers from succumbing to our unfortunate destiny, if we didn't find our mates. When Katrina came looking for me, I felt the relief of not having to fight my nature any longer, the relief of not having my brothers kill me because of my weakness. Katrina admires my strength— my perseverance, but she doesn't know that most of that stubbornness to not succumb was because of my desperate need to find my mate and find the happiness that I knew only my mate could give me.

Katrina isn't a pushover; if anything, she's stubborn and strong willed, but she is perfect to me. It is unexplainable, the all-consuming feeling of love that I hold for her, or the soul wrenching need I have to protect her from anything that could possibly want her harm. I know that I can control myself in any situation except one, where my woman might be threatened. If anyone tries to harm Katrina in any way, I won't hold myself responsible for the havoc that I can bring down on them.

"What's wrong?" I see Katrina looking up at me with a frown on her face, she is sensing the anger in my thoughts.

"Nothing." Lowering my head, I kiss her lips, "nothing at all." She places her hand over my heart, stroking my chest with her thumb. She looks at me with concern in her eyes before nodding and turning so we can continue on our way.

"Thought you lovebirds were going to sleep the morning away," Tor calls out as we enter the bar area to find him near the outside door, talking to Colburn. By his tight features and stiff body, I would say that something is angering him. Whatever it is, I will have to ask him, because if he was going to tell me he would have done so already.

"Why don't you go get yourself some coffee? I think Gabriella has been in the kitchen because I can smell something sweet."

Katrina eyes me curiously, then smiles. "You don't need to tell me twice." She turns to leave just as Tor reaches us.

"Where are you going, Beautiful? Running away from me already?"

Katrina glances over her shoulder and winks, before making her way towards the kitchen.

"What's up?" Tor inclines his head towards the outside door before he turns and starts making his way outside. Walking next to him, we make it to the parked bikes before he starts talking. "This whole mess with Dag's woman is blowing up." Turning his back to me, he lifts his hands to draw his fingers through his long-unbound hair. Dag realized from a photo he saw that his woman was on the run from one of Cape Town's most dangerous gangs. When we started looking for her, war was declared between the Elementals and the Desperados, as Sean, the gang's leader, was adamant that we should keep away from her, but as she is Dag's woman it's impossible for us to ignore that fact and turn away.

We then found out that Dag's woman, Esmeralda, had stolen a ledger from Sean. We later got our hands on that ledger and managed to get rid of Sean, but the gang hasn't desisted from looking for the woman, which leaves Dag desperate to find her and bring her in to safety, but I think she is making it difficult for him.

"They have acquired the help of the Spitting Cobras." He snaps around, his body now vibrating with pent-up anger. Tor had a run in with one of the Cobras a few years back, ever since then, he would be happy to obliterate them, but the problem is, the Cobras have the cops in their pockets, they can make our life difficult when it comes to the law.

"How do you know?" Tor shrugs at my question as he leans against one of the bikes. "One of the motherfuckers dropped a present at the gate. It was an or *else* type of gift."

I raise my brow. "They got hold of one of our men?" If any fucker touches any of our men, they will be dead. I can feel the anger coursing through my body.

"No, they grabbed Monica, our Jezebel, and beat her up, then dropped her off at the gate." A woman? They dared to touch a woman under our protection?

"Why wasn't she protected?" Now I know why Tor wasn't telling me, because he knows that I would lose my shit if they let one of the women from the club out unprotected when they are supposed to be on lockdown.

"She was fucking protected. She said she needed to go to the dentist, so Eirik took her. The problem is that she went in, but she never came out."

"They got her inside?" That means that they knew that she was coming.

Tor nods his head.

"Have you questioned her?"

"She says she went in but never made it to the dentist as a man accosted her outside the room doors."

"Does she know what he looked like?"

"No, but she saw his tattoo, and it was a Cobra."

I nod, we protect those in our care. Monica is one of the Jezebels in Tor's clubhouse. If someone attacked her, they will pay.

"We retaliate, if they attack one of ours. We make them remember that we are not to be messed with."

Tor nods and then inclines his head towards a Harley near the garage doors.

"Dag goes out every single night to find her, he has communicated with her sometimes. The info Celmund sent through, had him in a rage because of what she has gone through." I can only imagine the rage that fills him, knowing that his woman has been mistreated her whole life in one way or another.

"She's a crafty one, when we think we're close she slips away."

I hear Katrina approaching, the smell of coffee reaching me. "You want to tell me where you are going tonight?" If Tor realizes what I have planned, he will never let me forget it.

"Nope."

"Here you go," Katrina says as she hands me a mug of coffee and then holds one out to Tor.

"Coffee for me?" Tor asks with a wink as he takes his cup.

"There is also cake, but all your men were already getting their slices, so I thought you must have had yours."

Tor's eyes widen. "What?" he roars. "They better not have finished the cake, or I'll be breaking some heads." Tor hurries into the club, leaving me shaking my head as I look at Katrina, knowing that she manipulated the situation to give us alone time.

"Were they even eating cake?" I ask

"Of course," she replies with an innocent look which has me chuckling at her subterfuge.

"Come on, let's start our day before Tor comes out and you have to come up with another excuse to have me to yourself."

I grin when she huffs in irritation. Holding my phone, I text Burkhart to know that we ready to leave. Katrina is mumbling to herself as she makes her way towards my Harley, which has me grinning. Drinking my coffee, I place the empty mug on the wall near the entrance before making my way towards my woman.

Turning Katrina towards me, I pull her hands away from the fastening on her helmet and tie it myself. "I thought that's why we came away this weekend, so I could have you all to myself." Lowering my head, I kiss her, quietening her anger.

"You have me all to yourself from now on," I whisper against her lips. She is right because the reason for bringing her here was to have time just for the two of us, but being in the club, I should have known that there would be things that catch my attention.

"This is so exciting." Glancing over my shoulder, I see Burkhart and Saskia approaching, his arm around her shoulders as they smile at each other. "Do you know where we are going?"

"No, Draco has kept as quiet as the tomb," Katrina mutters under her breath.

"It's supposed to be a surprise," Burkhart intervenes, "you ladies don't want to mess up the surprise, now do you?" Saskia backhands him on the stomach with a grin on her face as she shrugs.

"All I know is that I'm with you, that's better than anything you could give me."

From the corner of my eye, I see Katrina smile and nod.

"Well, if that's the case then we might as well stay here for Tor's party, as you will be with me, so no need to continue with this surprise." Saskia looks up at Burkhart, shaking her finger at him.

"No, we wouldn't want that after all the effort to get us he…" she stops talking as Burkhart takes the index finger she's waving around into his mouth, sucking at it gently.

I hear her sigh, which has me grinning as I look at Katrina and see her shaking her head with amusement on her face. "You guys are all the same," she states.

"Me? I'm nothing like that." I hold back a chuckle at her raised brow. Lifting my hand, I stroke my thumb over her bottom lip, my eyes following the motion.

"You see what I mean, you were the teacher," she quips just as she opens her mouth and bites my thumb. Not hard enough to hurt, but enough to have me throw back my head and chuckle at her cheekiness.

"Minx." I playfully slap her ass which has her gasping as I sit on the Harley, straightening it I look at my woman, "Get on!"

"You know, if you weren't so easy on the eyes, I wouldn't let you get away with half the things I let you get away with." Her words reach me as we make our way onto the road, Burkhart riding just to my right. I grin, knowing that it wasn't the way I looked that attracted Katrina when we first met, if anything it put her off as she figured me for a player.

Celmund sent me a text last night to let me know that everything is on track. We shall go for breakfast near the ocean, and then for a long ride stopping to see the scenery, before making our way towards the Hotel. There we will be having dinner in their Michelin Star restaurant, but before that happens two suites have been booked for Katrina and Saskia to change.

We have purchased two ball gowns, one for my woman and another for Saskia. Today I want it to be all about Katrina.

KATRINA 6

Today has been really great. Even though Burkhart and Saskia are with us, it has been mostly Draco and I doing our thing and Burkhart and Saskia doing theirs. It is the first time since we mated that I have seen Draco doing nothing but just relaxing with me. We had breakfast at a rustic little bakery overlooking the ocean. Draco video called Bion, and we got to see and talk to Damon.

Even though Draco acts all macho, I can tell that he was missing Damon, too. After our call, we went on a long ride, stopping in different little villages to look around. Now we're at a five-star hotel. When we walked in, I was sure that security was going to ask us to leave by the way they were looking at Draco and Burkhart, but when Draco confirms his reservation, I see the surprise on the receptionist's face.

I understand what the surprise is about when we are taken to the suites. "Oh." That is all I can say for now as I look around. The room is fabulous, I have never been in such a rich, comfortable room.

"Draco?" I glance over my shoulder at him to see his smile. He slides his arms around my waist, pulling my back against his chest.

"I want it to be perfect for you today, so go on in, that box on top of the bed is a dress for you to put on." I look over at the huge bed to see a big square box in the middle of the bed. The excitement I feel at what Draco has prepared is rushing through my veins. I can't wait to see the dress in the box. He lowers his head, kissing my shoulder before letting go of my waist.

"I'll be back in a couple of minutes; I know that you like to dress up without me around." I can't wait to see what Draco got me. Turning, I slide my arms around his shoulders, gliding my fingers into his hair as I raise up on my tiptoes and kiss his sweet lips.

"Thank you. Today has been amazing, and I am very blessed to have found you." he takes my lips in a loving kiss that has me wanting to curl up against him and just spend the rest of the night with Draco. When he finally lifts his head, I'm ready to get undressed and jump into bed with the love of my life and my son's father, but he steps back.

"Don't tempt me woman, go get ready." And with those words he turns and leaves, which has me huffing in irritation as I turn towards the bed. Well, I might as well go and see what he got me, so I can see what else he has planned for the evening. When I open the box, I gasp at the shimmering, dark blue silk dress that lays inside. Pulling the dress carefully out of the box, I squeal in happiness, admiring the dress Draco got me.

Whatever we are doing tonight must be fancy. This is the kind of dress that you wear for special occasions. I wish I had time to run a bath and just lie in there for half an hour or so before it's time to leave. But because I have no idea what is planned, I better start getting ready now. Rushing into the bathroom to take a quick shower, I stop, a smile splitting across my face.

On top of the bathroom counter is my makeup bag. Somehow, Draco must have got one of the prospects to bring it here while we were away. Pulling the clip for my hair out of my makeup bag, I tie my hair up into a loose bun as I wash my face. If Draco went through all this trouble to make today perfect, then I will make an effort to blow his socks off.

After applying my makeup, I let my hair down, the auburn tresses falling around my shoulders. One thing that Draco loves about me is the color of my hair. Pulling my fingers through the loose curls, I make sure my hair is knot free before walking into the room to slip the stockings up my legs.

When I pick up the dress I smile, I can't wait to see how it's going to look. Pulling the dress up over my hips, I slide my arms into the little spaghetti straps before arranging the dress over my curves and sliding the zip up.

Leaning down, I slip my feet into the beautiful strappy high heel shoes he also left me. Walking towards the floor to ceiling mirror, I smile. Draco, hold on, because I'm going to blow your eyeballs out tonight. I make my way towards the sitting room to look out the window while I wait. I don't wait for long before Draco is opening the door to the room. Turning, I see him step in before he stops.

"What do you think?" He is just standing there, his eyes roaming over my body, his muscles stiffening. "Well, I guess I made you speechless." One minute he is standing there staring by the door, the next he has his hands at my waist, and he is lifting me off the floor.

"You are the most beautiful woman I have ever seen." His voice is low, his blue eyes intense.

"That is saying something, seeing as you have lived for centuries," I tease as I slide my arms around his shoulders before touching my lips to his. The kiss is meant to be sweet, but it turns out to be scorching hot.

Burkhart's voice has me gasping in surprise as I lift my head at his words. "Maybe you should have closed the door, Brother."

Draco lowers his forehead to my breasts, groaning. "I swear, one day I'm going to kill you," Draco's voice rumbles as he slowly lowers me to my feet.

Smiling, I slide my arms down his chest as I touch the ground. "Shall we go?" I ask innocently, which has Draco scowling over his shoulder at Burkhart as I step around him.

"Looking beautiful, sweetheart," Burkhart says with a wink.

Draco growls deep in his chest. "Weren't they just great? That dress is beautiful," I compliment, approaching Saskia that is looking beautiful in a red dress.

"So, is yours, do you know yet where we are going?" I shake my head. Now that I'm dressed up, I am glad to be surprised because it seems like Draco has put a lot of thought into this day. Draco places his hand on my lower back, guiding me out of the door and towards the lift. We make our way to the ground floor and I notice that Draco and Burkhart are still wearing their low-cut jeans and kutte's. I hope that wherever we are going, they allow them inside dressed in jeans.

Walking out of the lift, the men guide us towards one of the lounges. The sign on the door indicates that a private function is in progress. Glancing over at Draco, I frown when he opens the door and steps inside. Well, it looks like the private party has something to do with us. When we walk inside, I hear Saskia gasp. There are twinkling lights all over, and two tables, one on each side of a dance floor. The tables have beautiful silver chandeliers with white candles burning.

Draco guides me towards one of the tables and I see that Burkhart and Saskia are sitting at the other table.

"Oh, my word, I can't believe you did all of this for me," I whisper, feeling tears fill my eyes.

Draco leans forward, his thumb stroking my cheek, cleaning a tear away. "No, I don't want you to cry or I will end this right here, and your surprise is nearly happening." I smile at him as another tear slides down my cheek. Draco hates seeing me cry. When I was in labor with Damon, I thought he was going to tear down the Infirmary in frustration in not being able to make my pain stop.

"I'm really happy, you have outdone yourself."

Draco winks at me just as I hear the first note.

I ride to find open spaces.

I ride where nobody has left their traces.

It's not to find familiar faces. Two wheels hand me the hope.

Pocket full of dreams, A couple of my schemes,

To feel sane when nobody else to blame.

So, bring me the highway, so I can do this my way.

One day or night, these eyes will close, and on the other side I will say, it's the life I chose.

I can't believe it! The minute I heard the first word, I knew it was Blue Strada. I have loved his music for as long as I can remember. His voice has a soothing tone in it that is incomparable. I hear Saskia from behind me shriek in pleasure. Turning towards where his voice is coming from, I see Blue himself sitting on a high stool with his guitar. He's wearing his signature torn jeans and T-shirt, that is what I also like about him. Even though he is popular, it doesn't seem like it goes to his head, as he maintains his down-to-earth personality.

From what I have read in magazines and the pictures I have seen of him; women throw themselves at him all the time. The man is handsome, not as handsome as Draco, but hot in his own way. I get the impression that even though he's got it all, he isn't happy. Looking back at Draco I see his eyes on me, I can't imagine how much he paid to get Blue to give us a private show.

"I can't believe you did this for me!" Placing my hand on his cheek, he turns his head to kiss my palm. Looking at Draco, no one would ever say that he could be so thoughtful, his animalistic energy has grown men fearing him. Blue is still singing, his voice involving us in an enchanted dream state of heartfelt emotions.

"You deserve this, and much more, but if you continue looking all moony over the fucker, I will have to end him."

I gasp, looking behind me to see Blue grin as he ends a song. "Shh, I think he heard you."

I know that Draco is possessive, but he should know by now that I have no interest in anyone except him.

"Draco." I jump in surprise when I hear Blue's voice sounding closer. Glancing over my shoulder I see him approaching, but suddenly my view is covered by Draco standing between us.

"Blue." Draco's voice is low, a warning clear in his voice.

"King says hi." They know each other? Why didn't Draco ever tell me that he knew Blue Strada?

"Thanks for doing this." I won't be hidden, I know that Draco doesn't like me near other men, but Draco is faster and stronger than anyone has a right to be, therefore, there is no reason for me to be hiding like a mouse behind his back. Standing, I take a step around Draco, his arm comes around my waist pulling me against him.

"Thank you so much for doing this; I have been a fan forever."

Turning slightly into Draco's embrace, I place my flat palm on his stomach.

"My pleasure. Any special requests?" I can feel Draco's body go rigid next to me, his blue eyes intense as he looks at Blue.

"All your son…" my sentence is cut short as all hell breaks loose. I'm suddenly flat on the ground with Draco above me, covering my body. Shots are being fired; his body is vibrating over me with his rage.

"Who the fuck is shooting?" Burkhart roars.

"Don't move until I tell you," Draco whispers near my ear. I nod to let him know that I heard. The hand he has next to my head lifts and I know that he will be bending one of his elements, but whoever had the bad idea of shooting at us won't be standing for long after attacking us.

"Your club thinks they can attack us without retaliation?" a man's voice is heard after another shot is fired.

"Are you fucking crazy, what the fuck?" Blue roars just as I hear a gurgling noise, then another shot is fired. Draco's weight is suddenly off me. Turning my head, I see him making his way towards a man that has been thrown against the main doors that we came in. Another is standing next to him, Blue and Burkhart on him. Blue is pulling back his fist before letting loose and punching the man. Draco is now before the man that is against the door, held by an invisible force.

"Are you okay, Katrina?" Saskia asks from where she's also laying on the floor. Lifting my head, I look over my shoulder to see her doing the same.

"I bet we will never have another Valentine's Day like this again," I mutter, only to hear Saskia start to laugh, which has me grinning at my own words.

Our camaraderie comes to a complete stop when I hear screams of pain.My eyes snap up to see Draco with his hand on the man's bicep. "Why the fuck would the Hades MC shoot at us?" Burkhart asks.

"Not...not you... the...the Wolverine MC." The man being held by Burkhart says.

"You are fucking with me, right? This is all blow back with the Wolverines?" Burkhart roars. "You messed up our plans for a fucking blow back that has nothing to do with us?"

"Sorry about these guys," Blue grunts as he pulls the guy forward and then pushes him hard against the door again. "I will get King to send someone to pick them up." It's a good thing that this lounge is soundproof because of the music they must play in here, or the hotel would be in a panic with the gunshots.

"Fuck you," The one by Draco grunts, but as soon as the words are out of his mouth he screams. Draco is burning the flesh on his arm, his hand tightening around his bicep.

"You say another word, and you won't be breathing again," Draco's growls.

His statement has the man paling.

Shaking my head, I pull up my dress slightly as I move to stand, grunting as I get onto my feet.

"Draco." My whisper has his head snapping around to look at me. "Let's go."

His scowl deepens, I know that he wanted to make today perfect. The fact that these men messed his plans will have him furious. I know that he will not leave easily, especially when these men shot at us and placed Saskia and me in danger. "Fine!" Turning, I look at Saskia that is patting down her dress. "Shall we go up to our rooms., Saskia?"

Saskia looks up at me with a frown then at the men. When her eyes catch mine again, I can see that she understands because she nods as she walks towards me. "Of course." Looking back at the men it is clear that we will never be able to get through those doors. Looking around I find the other exit doors by the stage.

"Katrina," there is a warning in Draco's voice, a warning that I'm not going to heed as I continue making my way towards the door. I know that if I stay, one of those men will probably die if they continue questioning them. The minute I touch the door to open it I am lifted off the floor, which has me gasping in surprise.

Instead of arguing, I keep quiet, knowing that Draco will not be in the mood to talk. Looking over my shoulder, I see Burkhart standing before Saskia, his back rigid as he glares down at her. The door closes behind Draco and me as he makes his way towards the lifts. Lowering my head to his chest, I close my eyes, listening to his heart beating. I know that people will be looking at us as he carries me across the foyer, but I don't care as I am being held close against Draco's heart.

When Draco closes the suite's door behind us, I open my eyes but don't talk. Draco stands without moving for a few minutes before he finally makes his way towards the couch and takes a seat, still holding me close. After a couple of minutes of silence, I finally lift my head to look at him.

"Thank you."

His frown deepens.

"No, don't get irritated because of how it ended." I take in a deep breath before sitting up. "You have once again shown me how very lucky I am to have such a wonderful, caring man as my mate. Draco, I love you with all my heart." Leaning forward, I kiss his lips. "You are my lover, my best friend, the father of my child, and the consuming soul bearing the love that completes me. Draco, thank you, it might not have gone the way you planned, but it was perfect, because you did all of this for me."

Draco lifts his hand, placing it on my cheek. His eyes, that magnetic blue, talks of deep emotions coursing through him. He pulls my face towards his until our lips are barely touching.

"I love you." They are just three little words, but coming from Draco, they mean everything. It has been a bloody

Valentine's Day, but one that has shown me how much my man truly cares and loves me.

THE END.

One Small Spanish Wish

ALORA 1

"Has anyone seen Alora?" I hear Kole say from inside the pub. Kole was the only one to give me a helping hand two years ago when I really needed it. Kole isn't always here as he travels between the many pubs that he owns, but even from far away he has the respect of all his staff that have in one way or another been touched by his kind heart. Kole and I are friends, he is the only person that knows about Jason.

At the memory of Jason, I tense, I don't know what is wrong with me today, but he keeps popping into my mind. I shake my head as if the image of the only man that I have ever loved will disperse like that. My ponytail swishing across my back as I open the door and step inside. "I'm here" I call and see Kole turn around to look at me. His green eyes taking in the dark circles under my eyes from lack of sleep and the tired look on my face.

"How's Jackson?" he asks as he approaches, Jackson is now a year and four months old and Kole's godson. Ever since the day that he found out that I was pregnant that he has done everything in his power to make sure that Jackson and I have everything we need. I don't know what I would have done without Kole when I first came to Cadiz looking for a new life.

"His fever has broken, and he was sleeping when I left." I leave Jackson with Mrs. Alverez, our neighbour and a kind and gentle Spanish woman that is a mother to three sons and two daughters. All her children are now out of the house and her husband died just a couple of years ago, which leaves Mrs. Alverez craving for something to do. She has taken to Jackson like one of her grandchildren, and Jackson loves her like a grandmother.

"Why don't you go home and take a few hours sleep while he's asleep too, it's fine we can make do today." I smile up at him, knowing very well that they would struggle with one less person. Christmas is just around the corner and everyone is in a party mood, the pub has been full every night, closing way after midnight. I would gladly stay home but firstly I don't want others to have to work extra because I'm home and secondly I need the extra cash that I make here at this time of year on tips to carry me through the holidays.

"I'm fine," I state as I place a hand on his arm, "now let me get to it because soon we will have the place crawling with tourists." I'm about to step around him when his words stop me.

"You are working on the alcoves today."

"Why?" I'm always on the open areas and usually let the newbies take the alcoves as they are quieter.

"You need to take it slower today, now stop arguing and get to it," he quips as he makes his way towards the bar. I shake my head at his back. The man is always looking out for others, it is time that someone soon starts looking after him. I turn, making my way towards the alcove areas, to be honest I can do with a slower pace today. I have a slight headache from the lack of sleep and my body is feeling lethargic, which isn't something I relish today.

People start arriving soon after I have made sure that everything is as it should be, and the rush begins. I am thankful for this job; it has kept me sane through some rough times. When I first arrived in Cadiz, I was full of dreams, dreams that soon vanished when reality set in. Jason told me to come here to meet him, that we would find a house and build a life together, but when I arrived there was no Jason and I had to try and build a life all by myself. I tried to phone Jason so many times but to no avail, I was in a strange city with nowhere to live and hardly any money to sustain myself. Kole found me crying in one of the alcoves, he offered me a job and a temporary place to live until I found my feet. When he found out that I was pregnant he helped me with everything, he was a Godsend. I would never have thought that Jason would have done that to me, but he did. I feel my heart tighten when I think of him, no matter how much time passes the hurt is still there as strong as ever.

I met Jason when I was working at the airport. Our romance seemed pure and real, but apparently, I was wrong, and no matter how much I try to forget him I can't as Jackson is the spitting image of his father. Jason has the silkiest black hair I have ever seen, his light green eyes hypnotic in his tanned face. At twenty-eight, Jason had the body that many women dream of in a man. I was twenty-three when he met me, and innocent to the ways of men, now at twenty-five I am cynical to any advances that I may get from any man.

I have had a few men ask me out, but I have always turned them down, I'm not ready to date, the mere thought of kissing someone else besides Jason has me cringing. It is stupid because Jason left me high and dry, not once worried that I didn't know anyone in a new city or that I didn't have a job to turn to. At the time I didn't know that I was pregnant, I found out a couple of days after starting here at the pub. I remember how devastated I was, first I lost the man that I thought had loved me and then I find out that I am pregnant with his child.

"Can I have another?" I come back to the present as I look at the man sitting at one of my tables. Smiling, I nod and turn to go and collect his drink. Maybe because of not sleeping, my mind is all over the place today, which isn't good when the pub is so busy. Walking past the huge

Christmas tree that we erected a couple of days ago, I smile seeing the lights twinkling.

I love Christmas, it's my favourite holiday. I just hope that I can give Jackson the Christmas that he deserves, because money is always tight when bringing up a little boy and paying for everything yourself. I look up to see a man sitting at the bar, at first I tense when I see his wide back and raven dark hair, my heart racing, but then he turns slightly and I see that it isn't Jason. Of course, it isn't you idiot, why would it be him when he doesn't even know where I am, and Cadiz is a very big city, even if he did try to find me I doubt he would.

"Antonio, another draught for table forty-six please." Antonio looks over his shoulder at me and nods.

"Is that his fourth one?" he asks in his broken English. At my nod he frowns, "you be careful, he might start giving you trouble." I look towards the table where the five men are sitting, the other four have been moderate with their drink but this one has been overdoing it slightly, I will have to keep an eye on him.

"I just sat a customer at table sixty-three," Jose says as he walks past me, picking up the draught I head towards table forty-six. "Here you go, Sir," I murmur as I place the draught before him.

"Aww sweetheart, don't call me sir. You make me feel ancient." He's not ancient, but he's older than me, I would say he's in his late forties. "Call me Tom," he says with a wink which I ignore, turning I make my way towards table sixty-three and my new customer. I hear Tom's friends laughing at his terrible try at flirting. Pulling my notebook out of my front black apron pocket, I turn to a new page as I make my way to the table.

"Hello, what can. . ." I feel like my heart has just stuttered and stopped as I look up and am caught in the magnetic green gaze. I can feel my hand shaking, my stomach tensing, and I swear if I had eaten anything recently, I would be sick.

"Alora," his deep husky voice drowning out the Christmas tunes that have been playing in the background. How did he find me? Why did he find me? He looks still the same, his presence vibrant with danger. I feel like crying, but I won't give this man the satisfaction of seeing what he did to me, instead I turn and walk towards the staff area. I hear him call my name again, but I ignore it, I can't deal with this right now. I'm only a couple of feet away from his table when I feel a hand tighten around my upper arm, my whole-body tenses at the touch.

"Wait, let me explain," he says from behind me.

"Let go of me." Is that my voice?

"Alora, just listen." I feel his fingers tightening, but I don't turn.

"Is there a problem here?" I look up to see Kole standing before us, his stance tenses, a scowl on his face.

"Keep out of this," Jason says, a note of danger in his voice.

"Alora why don't you take a break?" Kole says, I feel Jason's fingers tense but then they release my arm which has me walking away without a backword glance. Why now?

JASON 2

"I'm not here to create any problems, I just want to speak to Alora." I have waited two long years to see her again and try to make amends, I won't be daunted by this guy before me or by her refusal to speak to me. Seeing her again was like the calm to the storm that has been brewing within me, Alora was the light in the darkness that was my life, but unfortunately that darkness touched us before I could vanquish it.

"Why, after so long?" I tense, how does this guy know about me? The thought that Alora might be with someone else has my whole-body tensing. I have been consumed by Alora, have been counting down the time that I would finally be joined with her again. To find her and then find out that she is with someone else drives a stake right through my heart.

"That is between her and me," I mutter.

"No, it isn't, I will make sure that you don't hurt her again. If you are genuine, I will help you, but if you are here to hurt her again, then you need to turn and leave." I respect someone that will stand up for those around them, but most importantly he has just told me that he will help me with Alora if I am genuine, which tells me that they are not together.

"I wasn't able to come for Alora until now, it wasn't for lack of trying." If he only knew how desperately I fought to get to her, but to no avail. Sometimes life imposes on the best laid plans, I never thought that I would find someone that would love me unconditionally and utterly but when I met Alora, I felt it and knew without a shadow of a doubt that she was mine. "I need to speak to her; I need to explain." I see the man before me trying to analyse my every word, trying to figure out if what I say is the truth.

In a sense I'm pleased that Alora has found someone that has looked out for her when I wasn't around, but in another sense I can feel the jealousy that another man was doing what I should be doing. That she now trusts him more than she does me. Alora was brought up in foster care. She has always been alone. One thing that constantly poked at my mind while I was away from her was how she always said how for the first time in her life she felt like she had someone that cared about her.

"There can't be an explanation for leaving a woman you profess to love in a new city without a roof over her head or a job, completely helpless." I can see the anger in the man's green eyes as he looks at me.

"I do love her, and if I could have been there I would." Fuck, if he only knew how much it has pained me knowing that I let the woman I love above everything else in this world down.

"Today is not a good time, and definitely not when she is working." The man says, "she is not going to want to talk to you."

"She has to listen; she needs to know that I didn't have an option. If I could have been by her side I would, this is the first opportunity that I had to come and look for her." I see the man look at my arm, his eyes on the tattoo. When they rise again to mine, there is a change in his expression which I can't read.

"Come back tomorrow at ten in the morning, but now I think you should leave." Everything in me rebels at the thought of not staying with Alora when I have finally found her again, but I also understand that she must be hurt, must be angry at the fact that I wasn't there when she came to meet me. I owe her everything and if I now need to give her a little time to acknowledge my presence, I will, but I will not go far.

"I will be here at ten." With those words I turn to leave, only to stop when the man places his hand on my shoulder.

"She has been hurt enough, if by any chance that is going to happen again then don't even come back, because you will have me to deal with then." I look at him; I'm not scared of his threats. After everything that I have seen and been through, I'm not scared of much, but I respect his loyalty to Alora.

"I will not hurt her again." He takes his hand off my shoulder and nods. I make my way out of the pub, but I won't go far, now that I have finally seen Alora I don't want to ever lose her again. Crossing the road, I slide into my metal grey Dodge Charger. Even though I can't see into the pub from here at least I know that she is in there which comforts me.

I have more money than I know what to do with it. After the two years of deep undercover I have resigned, wanting to make a life with Alora. I left two weeks before we were supposed to meet in Cadiz; I had to go in for some intel that I was gathering. Unbeknown to all of us, the Sicilian Mafia Boss took a shining to me, which complicated my extraction without alerting them to the fact that the government had someone in the inside of their organization.

These last two years have been wrought with crime, but I managed to acquire enough intel on the whole organization to bury the main players deep in a hole where they will never see sunlight again. I couldn't get any messages out or leave to come to Cadiz to find Alora. Also,

I didn't want to run the risk of someone finding out about her and hurting her to get back at me.

The Mafia think that I am dead but I run the risk of someone seeing me if I remain in Spain, I need to convince Alora that I was true to her all this time and take her with me wherever she wants to move to. I have made no plans since the extraction, instead I have placed all my energy in finding the woman that I love.

After the marines it was the natural progression for me to go into the CIA when I was offered the position, I never thought that I would have met someone like Alora, I was finishing an assignment at the time but that assignment prolonged into two years of hell. The Sicilian Mafia think that I died trying to stop the downfall of their kingpin but the truth is that I asked for an extraction after all the evidence was submitted. Even though they tried to convince me against it I have had enough. I have given enough of my life for my country, it is now time to enjoy my life with the woman that completes me.

I sit outside the pub until I see them start to switch off the lights. It is now past midnight but there are still a lot of people walking the streets as it's close to Christmas and most people are buying presents for their loved ones. I know that Christmas is Alora's favourite time of the year and I wanted to share it with her, but after her reaction earlier on I wonder if she will ever let me close to her again.

When our eyes clashed and I saw the deep hurt in hers. It was like a vice twisting at my heart. To know that I have hurt the person who I most cherish is like an open wound that just won't heal. I promise to try to make up for this lost time for the rest of my life if she will just give me another chance. The main door to the pub opens and two of the staff walk out talking among themselves. Alora is right behind them, but her head is down, and she is completely oblivious to what they are talking about. Then I see her stop, her head rises, and she turns just as the man I spoke to earlier appears in the doorway.

There is an exchange of words between the two of them, and then she once again turns to make her way to the exterior of the building. She must have parked her car at the back, I wait a couple of minutes, but I don't see a car. "Where the hell are you?" I mumble. The parking lot is deserted. Did someone maybe accost her when she was making her way to her car? The thought has me out of my car and walking towards where I saw her heading before I can think better of it. Walking around the building I stop, there are no cars parked behind here except for a black four by four which I'm guessing belongs to the guy that I suspect owns the pub.

Where the hell did she disappear to, and then I see a gate in the corner of the wall at the back, walking towards the gate, I realize that it leads to a back street. "Fuck," I mutter angrily, where the hell did you disappear to?

She must live close by, but there are various houses and apartments in this street which will make it impossible to find out at this time, but tomorrow I will know where she lives and if she isn't at work at ten, then I will find her and I will make her hear me out. I can see the Christmas trees through the windows twinkling at the passer-by's and wonder if Alora has one such tree in her window. When we first met, she once told me that she would love to have a big family, a family that she never had, a family that she can share Christmas with. I want to give her that; I want to be able to share the magic of Christmas with her.

I raise my hand and touch the pocket of my black leather jacket; my whole future depends on Alora's acceptance of my explanation. I know that she loved me once, the question is, does she still love me now or did that love change to hate?

ALORA 3

Looking down at Jackson's crib, I feel a tear streaking down my cheek. My heart feels so tight I feel like I can't breathe. His closed eyes hiding the dazzling green like his father. "Why?" I whisper, why would he come back now? To see him before me was like a dream come true until the truth of what he did crashed into my mind. After so long, why would he come to find me? What does he want from me?

Leaning down I stroke a finger gently over Jackson's fluffy tufts of black hair, a sad smile lifting my lips, I was starting to get used to waking up every morning knowing that Jason was not in my life and now out of the blue he comes back. When our eyes met, I felt the same friction coursing through my body like I always felt before when he used to look at me. Jason made me feel like no one else has ever made me feel, I was sure that he loved me, that he wanted me and only me. I was naïve and believed in the first man that showed me attention. I don't regret having Jackson, I can never regret having him. If it weren't for my little boy, I don't know if I would have been able to keep sane.

Jackson has kept me together; he has given me the strength to fight, the strength to hold it together. I will do anything for my little boy and that I will always be thankful to Jason for being part of it. Turning I walk to my bed, I don't have much money so I have to do what I can with the money I get from the pub. I pay rent, pay Mrs. Alverez for looking after Jackson and food. There isn't much left after that except for the tips, that is what I use to buy extras such as Jackson's clothes. I know that Kole pays me more than the others and I am eternally grateful, but I feel guilty and therefore try to compensate with the time I put in.

I don't spend as much time as I want to with Jackson, but one day, he will understand that to survive I have to work the hours that I do. After showering I stretch out under the covers, I know that now that Jason has seen me, he will be back, one thing I know about him is how stubborn he is. He said he wanted to talk; I know that he won't give up until we have talked. I need to be strong; I need to be able to keep my poise, I can't show him how much he hurt me, I can't let him know about Jackson.

Closing my eyes, all I can see is Jason's face, all I can feel is his fingers holding my upper arm. I lift my hand, rubbing the area gently, but I can still feel the warmth of his touch like a brand. A tear slips from the corner of my closed lid. All I wanted was one small wish for Christmas, to give Jackson a good Christmas, one that he would enjoy, one that would show him that magic really existed.

I must have fallen asleep because the next thing I know I am being awaken by Jackson's baby talk. Turning my head, I see him sitting in his cot, his chubby little hands waving in the air. "Morning sweet pea." As soon as he hears my voice, a sweet smile lights up his face.

"Mama, mama," his sweet voice makes me smile.

"Are you hungry, baby?" I ask as I sit up.

"Mama," he lifts himself against the bars, wiggling them excitedly.

"I'm coming, I'm coming," I murmur as I stand, walking towards him I pick him up burying my face against his shoulder. His little arms go around my neck as he nuzzles against me, which lightens my heart slightly. His beautiful light eyes shinning in happiness, reminding me so much of his father when we used to lay in bed for hours making love and teasing each other.

After spending the morning with Jackson, I get ready for work, I haven't been able to eat anything today worried that Jason might turn up again. Dropping Jackson off I head towards the pub, I found an apartment a block away from the pub which is handy and cheap as I don't have to pay transport. Opening the back door, I walk in to see Kole carrying a keg. "Morning, do you ever rest?" I ask walking past Kole towards the staff room.

"No, too much to do," he answers, "how is my godson?" I stop looking back at him and see a concerned frown on his face, I turn fully towards him again.

"He's okay, and he let me sleep," I say with a smile, but his expression doesn't change. "Are you okay?"

"I'm fine, its you that I'm worried about. We didn't have a chance to speak last night. How are you?" I don't know how to answer him, so I shrug. Ever since waking up this morning that I have tried to block out the thought of Jason, but unfortunately, he isn't a memory that likes to be repressed. "Do you want to know what he has to say?"

"I don't know, what he could possibly say that would make up for what he did two years ago?" I can hear the pain in my voice. Ever since I arrived in Cadiz that I have thought about every possible excuse for Jason, but none of them seemed plausible.

"Maybe you should listen to him, give him a chance to explain," Kole says as he comes to stand before me, I can feel the tears behind my eyes as I think of the useless excuses Jason will give me.

"I don't know," I murmur as I lower my head, Kole takes my hand and squeezes it gently before stepping away and back towards the cellar. I walk towards the staff room, opening the door I walk in and then freeze. My heart races at finding Jason sitting on one of the benches, Kole must have known that Jason was in here.

"Alora," his voice sends shivers down my back; I can feel my heart racing, but my feet are frozen in place. "Please just listen to me."

"Why?"

"Because I need to tell you why I wasn't there for you," he says as he throws up his hands in a plea.

"You look fine to me, so I gather you weren't killed," I say sarcastically. That was one of my greatest worries throughout the years that he somehow had been in an accident and died or something as drastic. I see the surprise on his face and then he stands, which has me taking a step back. His muscular body throbbing with pent-up energy.

"I'm sorry, I'm sorry that I wasn't there, I'm sorry that you struggled when you got here." His voice is hoarse with emotion, but being sorry doesn't make up for everything I went through when I first got here.

"You think that saying sorry will make up for what I went through?" I ask, my anger blooming at his words.

"No, that is why I need to explain to you," he says, taking another step towards me. I can't retreat anymore, which has me tensing. If he touches me, I will break down. Something that I do not want to do before him. "When you met me, I was on a job." His words surprise me, which has me raising my hands in question.

"I know, you told me that you had to come back because of a meeting you had." One thing that I always thought we had was the ability to talk, but I was wrong about everything else therefore I wouldn't put much faith in this, he was more than likely lying then too.

"Meeting?" I see his eyebrows rise in memory and then he nods, "Yeah you could say that." He lifts his hand, entwining his fingers through his hair. "I didn't tell you the truth before." I thought it wouldn't hurt but I was wrong, it still hurts. I turn to leave; I have heard enough but before I can open the door Jason has his hand flat on the door stopping me from opening it.

"Get out of my way," I say angrily.

"Just let me finish, you can tell me to leave afterwards." I can feel his presence right behind me, his voice close to my ear, my heart feeling tight, feeling betrayed. His body against my back as he places his other hand flat on the door, caging me in. My body feels like it will snap at any moment, every fibre, every cell is vibrating with his nearness.

"I was working undercover, when I came back, I was supposed to get some information I needed and leave, but things got complicated."

"What?" I snap around, completely forgetting his nearness. "This is what you are going with?" I see him tense at my words. "You really think that I'm going to believe this story?" I lift my hands and try to push at his chest, but he doesn't budge.

"It's not a story, I have been working undercover for four years, but when I met you, I thought that we were done with our assignment. We were wrong." His eyes are intense as he looks at me, "I tried to get out, but I was in too deep, they could not extract me at the time." He looks sincere but how can I believe him after what he did before? He lied to me even then, he could have just told me the truth and I would have waited.

"And you couldn't have phoned?" I ask raising my chin in anger, "why didn't you stay away? I don't need you here complicating my life again." I can see a flicker behind his eyes. At first it looked like it could have been pain, but I might be mistaken.

"I tried but you need to understand that where I was everything gets checked, they are suspicious and if I had even for a second given them a shadow of a doubt, then my cover would have been blown." He takes a step back and throws his hands up in frustration. "Do you really think that I didn't think about what was happening to you, I sent a message to the apartment you lived in, hoping that you would have got it but only when the assignment ended did I find out that you had already left when I sent the message. If they ever found out about you, your life would have been in danger."

"Why should I believe you?" I ask, my heart wants to believe him but my head refuses to accept his story.

"I have thought about you every single day, you know that what we have is special and you know that I would never stand you up if I could have stopped it." His words just make me angry.

"Do I?" I ask angrily, "I thought it was, but you showed me that it was just a lie."

"Dammit woman," suddenly his hands are once again on the door and his lips are over mine, the familiarity of his touch hitting me like a two-tonne truck. All the memories come flooding back, his touch, his smell, the overwhelming feeling of completeness that only he can give me.

"Sto. . ." I try to stop him when he lifts his head, but he then kisses me again, this time a blistering kiss that leaves me breathless.

"It has always been you, only you." His voice is low, urgent.

"I was alone, no job, no money and no you," I whisper, the tears finally overflowing. "You broke me, I won't let you do it again with your sweet words." I can see the look of pain on his face as he steps back, a pale look on his face.

"I would never hurt you, not purposefully." He takes a step away and then turns, "Alora you need to believe me," I wish I could, I really do but now I have Jackson to think of and I will not place myself or my son in the same vulnerability that I was before.

"No, I don't." I want more than anything to believe in him, I would like nothing more than to have him back in my life, but only a miracle will make me trust him again.

"What can I do for you to believe me?" he asks.

"I don't know Jason," I can hear the pain in my voice, a pain that has been etched ever since the moment that I found out I was pregnant and the man I loved wasn't there like he said he would be.

JASON 4

"I need your help." I heard one of the waiters talking and I now know he is called Kole, and the owner of this pub. Kole looks up at me and then frowns, I see his muscles tensing.

"I've already helped you by letting you talk to Alora, give it up." He crosses his arms as he stands before me. Being in the business that I was in has taught me not to be afraid of anyone, as life is way too short as it is.

"I need to prove to her that what I say is true."

"I can't see why any man would leave his woman stranded, that is not a simple mistake." Every muscle in my body tenses, I know that he is trying to protect Alora but knowing that I was responsible for her pain has me ticking like a bomb. "Look, you spoke to her two days ago and nothing changed, its Christmas soon, you want to make it right you show her that she can depend on you, that you're not going to disappear again."

"That is what I want to do, but she hasn't been at work."

"I'll tell you what, I am leaving tomorrow so if you can show me before I leave that you are here to stay then I'll help you." Shit, I can easily get all the information I need for Alora and I won't need him to tell me, but for some reason I think if I have him on my side that Alora will be more open to listening to me than if I ambush her. I look around to see if any of the staff is close, when I am certain that they are all far from prying ears I pull out the envelope I have in the inside of my jacket.

"Fine, I will show you that I am genuine, but the reason for me not making an appearance before, I'm afraid that is between Alora and me, and I have already told her the truth. Some things in here will prove to her that I spoke the truth." I open the envelope, looking through what I want to show him as the information about my undercover mission I will not share with this man or anyone else except Alora. "This should prove to you that I have good intentions towards my woman."

I see Kole lift a brow at my choice of words, but he doesn't say anything as he takes the papers and looks down at them. "You are taking a lot for granted, aren't you?" he says as he looks up at me again. "What if she decides that she doesn't want to give you a chance?" I point to the papers still in his hand.

"That there won't change, I owe her that and much more." He nods as he hands the papers back to me.

"I will give you her address, but I think you should maybe give her some kind of warning that you're coming," Kole says as he pulls out his phone and starts typing, "what's your number?" he asks.

After receiving the text with Alora's home address he places his hand on my shoulder. "Do right by her," with those words he turns making his way to the back.

"Thanks," I call out, which has him raising his hand but not turning. I place the envelope back in my pocket before looking down at Alora's address on my phone. She might not want to speak to me, and think that all is lost but I will not rest until she realizes that I love her and I will do everything in my power to make her happy and show her for the rest of my life that she is the most important person in the world for me.

I head towards my car and Alora. Tomorrow is Christmas, a season that should be magical and happy full of love and dreams. A season that Alora has always loved. I want to make this Christmas the happiest one for her, I will fight for us even though she thinks there is no us, and I will show her that I can be dependable even if it takes the rest of my life.

Arriving outside her apartment building, I look up to see a nicely maintained building, with only six apartments in the building. I step out of the car and make my way towards the main building door when I see a woman that must be in her sixties opening the door. Rushing towards the door I hold it for her which has her looking up from the pram she's pushing and smile at me.

"Gracias," she says with a smile as she walks past.

"Es un placer," I reply, one reason why I was considered for the job that I had was because of my fluency in Spanish. Ignoring the lift I climb the stairs to the second floor, turning to my left I look at Alora's door, I smile as I can hear Christmas music coming from inside, approaching I knock waiting as I hear movement inside.

"Did you forge. . ." Alora starts to say before she sees me, then her complexion pales and she tries to shut the door.

"Wait," I say as I place the palm of my hand on the door stopping her from closing it. I can see what looks like panic on her face as she glances behind her. Is she hiding something, has she found someone else and doesn't want to tell me? I know it's unreasonable, but I can feel the anger rising within me as I push the door open, which has her taking a step back involuntarily. My eyes travel around the area seeing a lounge that is sparsely furnished with one couch, a small Christmas tree and a Television that has been mounted on the wall.

Turning my head I see a door that leads into a small kitchen that seems to be empty, unless there is someone in the bedroom, which doesn't seem like it as I'm sure they would have come out by now.

"How did you find me?" she asks as she places a hand to her chest, "You shouldn't be here."

"I want to show you that I mean what I say, and that everything I told you is true," I say as I step inside and close the door behind me.

"No, you should leave," she says as she again looks around.

"After I have shown you what I came here to show you, then if you want me to leave I will but I will warn you that I am not going to give up." I see her shoulders slump in defeat as she nods.

"Fine, but I'm busy so please make it quick." I frown when I sense her anxiety. Something isn't right, but I can't put my finger on it.

Nodding I pull the envelope out of my pocket, "I have brought you evidence that what I said to you is true." I lift some papers and hand them to her, I have purposefully covered names so that she can never be accused of knowing something that she shouldn't, but I have added a couple of photos that will show her that what I say is true. I have also added some communication between my counterintelligence officer that will show her I have been working the case. She looks down at the papers, I see her scanning through them, when she picks up the first photo she frowns and then looks up at me.

"You look different somehow," she says.

"I had to integrate, to do that I needed to become one of them." She nods.

"Are you still doing this?" she says as she lifts her hand.

"Am I still in intelligence?" I ask and see her nod as she looks at another photo.

"Yes, but I won't be working undercover." She looks up at me with pain in her eyes, I would give anything to wipe the pain away, but I can't, the only thing I can do is try to make up for it. "I want a normal life, a life with you."

"How can I trust you, how can I know that what you did won't happen again?" she says as she shakes her head. I hand her the other papers that I have in my hand, papers that I hope will show her that I want her and that I will do anything to keep her.

"I hope that will show you that I mean what I say." She looks down at the papers and then I see her tense and her head snaps up.

"What's this?"

"Exactly what it says," I say with a shrug. "I would have preferred you to choose it with me, but I think you will like that house." I found a beautiful three-bedroom house near the beach in Greece, I placed the house in Alora's name, so she knows that I mean what I say.

She looks back down at the papers in her hands and then frowns, "but this says Greece." I was hoping to broach this subject later once she accepted my intentions, but I might as well get this out of the way.

"I can't stay in Spain, the guys I brought down think I died, and they need to continue thinking like that. I was supposed to have left as soon as the main guys went down, but I can't leave without you." I see her eyes fill with tears.

"I can't do this again Jason, my life is here now, I'm not going to drop everything like I did before." She shakes her head, handing me the papers back, but I don't take them. Instead, I place my hand on her elbow and pull her against me. The papers crumple against us. I hear her gasp in surprise, but I don't let her complain as I cover her lips with mine. The feel of her soft body against mine has me hard and wanting. This woman can turn me on with a simple look, she is the sexiest, most alluring woman I have ever known. In the time that I haven't seen her, her body seems to have matured somehow.

Her beautiful breasts seem slightly more bountiful, her body womanlier if that is possible. I let go of her elbow, my hand moving up her arm to her jaw. I kiss her with everything in me, with all the passion, all the love that I feel for her. At first she fights it, but finally she lets go and kisses me back, the papers fall to the floor as her hands move up and around my neck. My hands draw down her body and under the short flowy dress that she has on, running up her silky legs until both hands are touching her bare ass cheeks.

I tighten my hold on her ass as I pick her up never breaking the kiss, her legs encircle my waist bringing her womanhood against my hardness. I can feel myself twitching against her with the need to be set free. I want to make love to her; I want to take my time with her, but it has been so long that I don't think this will take long at all.

Walking towards the couch I sit her on the back rest, her legs maintain their hold around me which allows for my hands to rise and free myself from the confines of my jeans. I stroke my cock once, before raising my hand to take one of hers that is around my neck and bringing it down to enclose me in her palm. The feel of her fingers around me has my knees weakening.

Grunting I finally break the kiss as I lower my head to her neck, kissing her there. The stroking of my member has my body tensing in beautiful torture. Lifting her dress to her waist, I pull her thong to the side and then I am pulling her hand away as I enter her scorching hot body.

"Ohh," she mumbles as I pull out and then thrust deeply, burying myself deep within her body. "Jason," she murmurs as her head falls back, giving me access to her beautiful neck. I want to stay like this forever, but we have been away from each other for way too long for this to last long. I can feel her body tensing around me as I quicken my pace.

"You so hot baby," I murmur as I lose myself completely in the act of making love to the only woman that can make me forget everything around me, that can brighten my day with her simple smile and that has been on my mind every day since the day I first saw her.

"Jas. . .Jason, ohh," she cries as her body tenses and then she is spasming around me, drawing out my orgasm, milking me of every drop of my essence. I thrust once more before stilling. Our breathing ragged as we try to calm it, try to calm our racing hearts.

"I love you baby; I know that it's hard to believe, but I love you with everything in me." I see a tear streak down her cheek as she opens her eyes and looks at me.

"I'm scared," she whispers which has my heart tightening in anger at myself, at the situation that had me hurt the woman I love.

"I know, but I promise that I will never leave you again." I pull back, missing her heat the moment our bodies separate.

"I cannot take the chance of it happening again." More tears streak down her cheeks, which has me leaning forward to kiss them away. Then I am leaning back as I place my hand in my outer jacket pocket and pull out the little box that I have there. I can feel the anxiety coursing through my body, I don't know what I will do if she says no.

Pulling back until her legs are sliding down the side of my body I step back as I help her stand, her dress falling into place, I arrange myself, buttoning up my jeans before I look at her to see her looking at me. Taking her left hand, I go down on my knee and see her frown until I lift the box and then her mouth opens in surprise.

"Oh," she murmurs.

"Please baby, will you marry me, will you agree to be my wife?"

"Jason," she whispers, "there is something you should know." I shake my head at her words.

"The only thing I need to know is if you still love me."

"Yes, but. . ."

"No buts baby, if you love me say yes and we can work out the rest later." I see the uncertainty in her face, but then she nods.

"Yes." My heart jolts in happiness when hearing the word that I have hoped for coming out of her mouth. Letting go of her hand I slip the ring out of the box and slide it onto her finger.

"I love you," I say as I kiss her finger with the ring, "this ring is just a display of my affection for you and I promise to make you happy." A tear runs down her cheek as she nods.

"I need to tell you something . . . " just then there is a knock on the door which has Alora tensing. Standing, I look at her as she pales. "Oh," she murmurs before she makes her way to the door.

"We got the icing," I hear a woman say in a broken English accent and then Alora is opening the door back and I see the lady that I opened the door for downstairs push the pram in as she walks in. When she sees me, she stops, looks at Alora and then back at me.

"Hello again," I say in English.

"Mama," my eyes snap down to the little voice and I freeze as I see the baby holding out its arms to Alora, "mama," he says again.

"Jason meet Jackson," Alora says as she leans down to pick up the baby that immediately wraps his arms around her neck as he places a wet kiss on her cheek. "Your son." To say I'm shocked is an understatement as I stand here frozen looking at a miniature mini me, not in my wildest dreams would I ever have thought that Alora was carrying my son and in a way it is good I didn't know because I would have done something stupid and placed the whole investigation in jeopardy.

"My son?" at my words she nods, looking down at Jackson, she points to me.

"Jackson, look, that's Daddy." The little boy turns its head. Our eyes meet and at that moment I fall in love all over again. Looking up, I see Alora's eyes filled with tears as she looks at me as she strokes the little boy's head.

"Thank you," I murmur as I approach. "Thank you for giving me a son, thank you for being the amazing woman that you are, the amazing mother that I see you have become, and I am so, so sorry that I wasn't there when Jackson was born." For the first time in a very long time, I feel tears choking me.

Stretching out my hand I touch Jackson's fingers gently, he looks at me suspiciously, his eyes the same exact colour as mine and then suddenly a toothless grin radiates from him and everything around me seems to once again come to rights.

"I guess you got an early Christmas present, Merry Christmas Daddy," Alora says. I look up at her. This beautiful, precious woman before me has given me the best Christmas I could ever wish for. I wanted to give her the best Christmas of her life, but it seems like I am the one that got a little miracle for Christmas, a miracle that I will cherish for the rest of my days.

THE END.

A MESSAGE FROM ALEXI FERREIRA

Thank you so much for reading Stormy Encounters. An introduction to these bad boy alphas, hope you enjoyed it. **If you enjoyed this book, please consider leaving a review. Reviews help authors like me stay visible and help bring others to my series.**

More books from Alexi Ferreira

ELEMENTAL'S MC SERIES

WULF (book 1)

BJARNI (book 2)

BRANDR (book 3)

CERIC (book 4)

BION (book 5)

CASSIUS (book 6)

CELMUND (book 7)

BURKHART (book 8)

CAELIUS (book 9)

DRACO SALVATION (book 10)

DRACO WRATH (book 11)

ELEMENTAL'S MC CHRISTMAS BLAST

ULRICH (book 1)

DANE (book 2)

DAG (book 3)

EIRIK (book 4)

TAL (book 5)

HALDOR (book 6)

WOLVERINE MC

BOUND (book 1)

TAMED (book 2)

STALKED (book 3)

REVENGE (book 04)

TEMPEST (book 05)

CHAOS (book 6)

BRATVA FURY SERIES

TORMENTED (book 1)

TURMOIL (book 2)

MAYHEM (book 3)

FURY (book 4)

BRING ME HER HEART (book 1)
BRING IT ALL DOWN (book 2)

BREATHING FIRE (book 1)

Printed in Great Britain
by Amazon

33135013R00185